GUY GARRICK

ARTHUR B. REEVE

1ST WORLD
LIBRARY
Literary Society

Guy Garrick

Arthur B. Reeve

© 1st World Library, 2009
PO Box 2211
Fairfield, IA 52556
www.1stworldlibrary.com
First Edition

LCCN: 2009923337

Softcover ISBN: 978-1-4218-8811-8
Hardcover ISBN: 978-1-4218-8910-8
eBook ISBN: 978-1-4218-8712-8

Purchase *"Guy Garrick"*
as a traditional bound book at:
www.1stWorldLibrary.com/purchase.asp?ISBN=978-1-4218-8811-8

1st World Library is a literary, educational organization
dedicated to:

- Creating a free internet library of downloadable ebooks

- Hosting writing competitions and offering book publishing
  scholarships.

1st World Library Literary Society

Giving Back to the World

"If you want to work on the core problem, it's early school literacy."

- James Barksdale, former CEO of Netscape

"No skill is more crucial to the future of a child, or to a democratic and prosperous society, than literacy."

- Los Angeles Times

"Literacy... means far more than learning how to read and write... The aim is to transmit... knowledge and promote social participation."

- UNESCO

"Literacy is not a luxury, it is a right and a responsibility. If our world is to meet the challenges of the twenty-first century we must harness the energy and creativity of all our citizens."

- President Bill Clinton

"Parents should be encouraged to read to their children, and teachers should be equipped with all available techniques for teaching literacy, so the varying needs and capacities of individual kids can be taken into account."

- Hugh Mackay

CONTENTS

CHAPTER I

THE STOLEN MOTOR

"You are aware, I suppose, Marshall, that there have been considerably over a million dollars' worth of automobiles stolen in this city during the past few months?" asked Guy Garrick one night when I had dropped into his office.

"I wasn't aware of the exact extent of the thefts, though of course I knew of their existence," I replied. "What's the matter?"

"If you can wait a few moments," he went on, "I think I can promise you a most interesting case—the first big case I've had to test my new knowledge of crime science since I returned from abroad. Have you time for it?"

"Time for it?" I echoed. "Garrick, I'd make time for it, if necessary."

We sat for several moments, in silence, waiting.

I picked up an evening paper. I had already read it, but I looked through it again, to kill time, even reading the society notes.

"By Jove, Garrick," I exclaimed as my eye travelled over the page, "newspaper pictures don't usually flatter people, but just look at those eyes! You can fairly see them dance even in the halftone."

The picture which had attracted my attention was of Miss Violet Winslow, an heiress to a moderate fortune, a debutante well known in New York and at Tuxedo that season.

As Garrick looked over my shoulder his mere tone set me wondering.

"She IS stunning," he agreed simply. "Half the younger set are crazy over her."

The buzzer on his door recalled us to the case in hand.

One of our visitors was a sandy-haired, red-mustached, stocky man, with everything but the name detective written on him from his face to his mannerisms.

He was accompanied by an athletically inclined, fresh-faced young fellow, whose clothes proclaimed him to be practically the last word in imported goods from London.

I was not surprised at reading the name of James McBirney on the detective's card, underneath which was the title of the Automobile Underwriters' Association. But I was more than surprised when the younger of the visitors handed us a card with the simple name, Mortimer Warrington.

For, Mortimer Warrington, I may say, was at that time one of the celebrities of the city, at least as far as the newspapers were concerned. He was one of the richest young men in the country, and good for a "story" almost every day.

Warrington was not exactly a wild youth, in spite of the fact that his name appeared so frequently in the headlines. As a matter of fact, the worst that could be said of him with any degree of truth was that he was gifted with a large inheritance of good, red, restless blood, as well as considerable holdings of real estate in various active sections of the metropolis.

More than that, it was scarcely his fault if the society columns had been busy in a concerted effort to marry him off—no doubt with a cynical eye on possible black-type headlines of future domestic discord. Among those mentioned by the enterprising society reporters of the papers had been the same Miss Violet Winslow whose picture I had admired. Evidently Garrick had recognized the coincidence.

Miss Winslow, by the way, was rather closely guarded by a duenna-like aunt, Mrs. Beekman de Lancey, who at that time had achieved a certain amount of notoriety by a crusade which she had organized against gambling in society. She had reached that age when some women naturally turn toward righting the wrongs of humanity, and, in this instance, as in many others, humanity did not exactly appreciate it.

"How are you, McBirney?" greeted Garrick, as he met his old friend, then, turning to young Warrington, added: "Have you had a car stolen?"

"Have I?" chimed in the youth eagerly, and with just a trace of nervousness. "Worse than that. I can stand losing a big nine-thousand-dollar Mercedes, but—but—you tell it, McBirney. You have the facts at your tongue's end."

Garrick looked questioningly at the detective.

"I'm very much afraid," responded McBirney slowly, "that this theft about caps the climax of motor-car stealing in this city. Of course, you realize that the automobile as a means of committing crime and of escape has rendered detection much more difficult to-day than it ever was before." He paused. "There's been a murder done in or with or by that car of Mr. Warrington's, or I'm ready to resign from the profession!"

McBirney had risen in the excitement of his revelation, and had handed Garrick what looked like a discharged shell of a cartridge.

Garrick took it without a word, and turned it over and over critically, examining every side of it, and waiting for McBirney to resume. McBirney, however, said nothing.

"Where did you find the car?" asked Garrick at length, still examining the cartridge. "We haven't found it," replied the detective with a discouraged sigh.

"Haven't found it?" repeated Garrick. "Then how did you get this cartridge—or, at least why do you connect it with the disappearance of the car?"

"Well," explained McBirney, getting down to the story, "you understand Mr. Warrington's car was insured against theft in a company which is a member of our association. When it was stolen we immediately put in motion the usual machinery for tracing stolen cars."

"How about the police?" I queried.

McBirney looked at me a moment—I thought pityingly. "With all deference to the police," he answered indulgently, "it is the insurance companies and not the police who get cars back—usually. I suppose it's natural. The man who loses a car notifies us first, and, as we are likely to lose money by it, we don't waste any time getting after the thief."

"You have some clew, then?" persisted Garrick.

McBirney nodded.

"Late this afternoon word came to me that a man, all alone in a car, which, in some respects tallied with the description of Warrington's, although, of course, the license number and color had been altered, had stopped early this morning at a little garage over in the northern part of New Jersey."

Warrington, excited, leaned forward and interrupted.

"And, Garrick," he exclaimed, horrified, "the car was all stained with blood!"

CHAPTER II

THE MURDER CAR

Garrick looked from one to the other of his visitors intently. Here was an entirely unexpected development in the case which stamped it as set apart from the ordinary.

"How did the driver manage to explain it and get away?" he asked quickly.

McBirney shook his head in evident disgust at the affair.

"He must be a clever one," he pursued thoughtfully. "When he came into the garage they say he was in a rather jovial mood. He said that he had run into a cow a few miles back on the road, and then began to cuss the farmer, who had stung him a hundred dollars for the animal."

"And they believed it?" prompted Garrick.

"Yes, the garage keeper's assistant swallowed the story and cleaned the car. There was some blood on the radiator and hood, but the strange part was that it was spattered even over the rear seat—in fact, was mostly in the rear."

"How did he explain that?"

Arthur B. Reeve

"Said that he guessed the farmer who stung him wouldn't get much for the carcass, for it had been pretty well cut up and a part of it flung right back into the tonneau."

"And the man believed that, too?"

"Yes; but afterward the garage keeper himself was told. He met the farmer in town later, and the farmer denied that he had lost a cow. That set the garage keeper thinking. And then, while they were cleaning up the garage later in the day, they found that cartridge where the car had been washed down and swept out. We had already advertised a reward for information about the stolen car, and, when he heard of the reward, for there are plenty of people about looking for money in that way, he telephoned in, thinking the story might interest us. It did, for I am convinced that his description of the machine tallies closely with that of Mr. Warrington's."

"How about the man who drove it?" cut in Garrick.

"That's the unfortunate part of it," replied McBirney, chagrined. "These amateur detectives about the country rarely seem to have any foresight. Of course they could describe how the fellow was dressed, even the make of goggles he wore. But, when it came to telling one feature of his face accurately, they took refuge behind the fact that he kept his cap pulled down over his eyes, and talked like a 'city fellow.'"

"All of which is highly important," agreed Garrick. "I suppose they'd consider a fingerprint, or the portrait parle the height of idiocy beside that."

"Disgusting," ejaculated McBirney, who, whatever his own limitations might be, had a wholesome respect for Garrick's new methods.

"Where did you leave the car?" asked Garrick of Warrington. "How did you lose it?"

The young man seemed to hesitate.

"I suppose," he said at length, with a sort of resigned smile, "I'll have to make a clean breast of it."

"You can hardly expect us to do much, otherwise," encouraged Garrick dryly. "Besides, you can depend on us to keep anything you say confidential."

"Why," he began, "the fact is that I had started out for a mild little sort of celebration, apropos of nothing at all in particular, beginning with dinner at the Mephistopheles Restaurant, with a friend of mine. You know the place, perhaps—just on the edge of the automobile district and the white lights."

"Yes," encouraged Garrick, "near what ought to be named 'Crime Square.' Whom were you with?"

"Well, Angus Forbes and I were going to dine together, and then later we were to meet several fellows who used to belong to the same upperclass club with us at Princeton. We were going to do a little slumming. No ladies, you understand," he added hastily.

Garrick smiled.

"It may not have been pure sociology," pursued Warrington, good-humouredly noticing the smile, "but it wasn't as bad as some of the newspapers might make it out if they got hold of it, anyhow. I may as well admit, I suppose, that Angus has

Arthur B. Reeve

been going the pace pretty lively since we graduated. I don't object to a little flyer now and then, myself, but I guess I'm not up to his class yet. But that doesn't make any difference. The slumming party never came off."

"How?" prompted Garrick again.

"Angus and I had a very good dinner at the Mephistopheles—they have a great cabaret there—and by and by the fellows began to drop in to join us. When I went out to look for the car, which I was going to drive myself, it was gone."

"Where did you leave it?" asked McBirney, as if bringing out the evidence.

"In the parking space half a block below the restaurant. A chauffeur standing near the curb told me that a man in a cap and goggles—"

"Another amateur detective," cut in McBirney parenthetically.

"—had come out of the restaurant, or seemed to do so, had spun the engine, climbed in, and rode off—just like that!"

"What did you do then?" asked Garrick. "Did you fellows go anywhere?"

"Oh, Forbes wanted to play the wheel, and went around to a place on Forty-eighth Street. I was all upset about the loss of the car, got in touch with the insurance company, who turned me over to McBirney here, and the rest of the fellows went down to the Club."

"There was no trace of the car in the city?" asked Garrick, of the detective.

"I was coming to that," replied McBirney. "There was at least a rumour. You see, I happen to know several of the police on fixed posts up there, and one of them has told me that he noticed a car, which might or might not have been Mr. Warrington's, pull up, about the time his car must have disappeared, at a place in Forty-seventh Street which is reputed to be a sort of poolroom for women."

Garrick raised his eyebrows the fraction of an inch.

"At any rate," pursued McBirney, "someone must have been having a wild time there, for they carried a girl out to the car. She seemed to be pretty far gone and even the air didn't revive her—that is, assuming that she had been celebrating not wisely but too well. Of course, the whole thing is pure speculation yet, as far as Warrington's car is concerned. Maybe it wasn't his car, after all. But I am repeating it only for what it may be worth."

"Do you know the place?" asked Garrick, watching Warrington narrowly.

"I've heard of it," he admitted, I thought a little evasively.

Then it flashed over me that Mrs. de Lancey was leading the crusade against society gambling and that that perhaps accounted for Warrington's fears and evident desire for concealment.

"I know that some of the faster ones in the smart set go there once in a while for a little poker, bridge, and even to play the races," went on Warrington carefully. "I've never been there myself, but I wouldn't be surprised if Angus could tell you all about it. He goes in for all that sort of thing."

"After all," interrupted McBirney, "that's only rumour. Here's

Arthur B. Reeve

the point of the whole thing. For a long time my Association has been thinking that merely in working for the recovery of the cars we have been making a mistake. It hasn't put a stop to the stealing, and the stealing has gone quite far enough. We have got to do something about it. It struck me that here was a case on which to begin and that you, Garrick, are the one to begin it for us, while I carry on the regular work I am doing. The gang is growing bolder and more clever every day. And then, here's a murder, too, in all likelihood. If we don't round them up, there is no limit to what they may do in terrorizing the city."

"How does this gang, as you call it, operate?" asked Garrick.

"Most of the cars that are stolen," explained McBirney, "are taken from the automobile district, which embraces also not a small portion of the new Tenderloin and the theatre district. Actually, Garrick, more than nine out of ten cars have disappeared between Forty-second and Seventy-second Streets."

Garrick was listening, without comment.

"Some of the thefts, like this one of Warrington's car," continued McBirney, warming up to the subject, "have been so bold that you would be astonished. And it is those stolen cars, I believe, that are used in the wave of taxicab and motor car robberies, hold-ups, and other crimes that is sweeping over the city. The cars are taken to some obscure garage, without doubt, and their identity is destroyed by men who are expert in the practice."

"And you have no confidence in the police?" I inquired cautiously, mindful of his former manner.

"We have frequently had occasion to call on the police for

assistance," he answered, "but somehow or other it has seldom worked. They don't seem to be able to help us much. If anything is done, we must do it. If you will take the case, Garrick, I can promise you that the Association will pay you well for it."

"I will add whatever is necessary, too," put in Warrington, eagerly. "I can stand the loss of the car—in fact, I don't care whether I ever get it back. I have others. But I can't stand the thought that my car is going about the country as the property of a gunman, perhaps—an engine of murder and destruction."

Garrick had been thoughtfully balancing the exploded shell between his fingers during most of the interview. As Warrington concluded, he looked up.

"I'll take the case," he said simply. "I think you'll find that there is more to it than even you suspect. Before we get through, I shall get a conviction on that empty shell, too. If there is a gunman back of it all, he is no ordinary fellow, but a scientific gunman, far ahead of anything of which you dream. No, don't thank me for taking the case. My thanks are to you for putting it in my way."

CHAPTER III

THE MYSTERY OF THE THICKET

"You know my ideas on modern detective work," Garrick remarked to me, reflectively, when they had gone.

I nodded assent, for we had often discussed the subject.

"There must be something new in order to catch criminals, nowadays," he pursued. "The old methods are all right—as far as they go. But while we have been using them, criminals have kept pace with modern science."

I had met Garrick several months before on the return trip from abroad, and had found in him a companion spirit.

For some years I had been editing a paper which I called "The Scientific World," and it had taxed my health to the point where my physician had told me that I must rest, or at least combine pleasure with business. Thus I had taken the voyage across the ocean to attend the International Electrical Congress in London, and had unexpectedly been thrown in with Guy Garrick, who later seemed destined to play such an important part in my life.

Garrick was a detective, young, university bred, of good

family, alert, and an interesting personality to me. He had travelled much, especially in London, Paris, Berlin, and Vienna, where he had studied the amazing growth abroad of the new criminal science.

Already I knew something, by hearsay, of the men he had seen, Gross, Lacassagne, Reiss, and the now immortal Bertillon. Our acquaintance, therefore, had rapidly ripened into friendship, and on our return, I had formed a habit of dropping in frequently on him of an evening, as I had this night, to smoke a pipe or two and talk over matters of common interest in his profession.

He had paused a moment in what he was saying, but now resumed, less reflectively, "Fortunately, Marshall, the crime-hunters have gone ahead faster than the criminals. Now, it's my job to catch criminals. Yours, it seems to me, is to show people how they can never hope to beat the modern scientific detective. Let's strike a bargain."

I was flattered by his confidence. More than that, the idea appealed to me, in fact was exactly in line with some plans I had already made for the "World," since our first acquaintance.

And so it came about that the case brought to him by McBirney and young Warrington was responsible for clearing our ideas as to our mutual relationship and thus forming this strange partnership that has existed ever since.

"Tom," he remarked, as we left the office quite late, after he had arranged affairs as if he expected to have no time to devote to his other work for several days, "come along and stay with me at my apartment to-night. It's too late to do anything now until to-morrow."

I accepted his invitation without demur, for I knew that he meant it, but I doubt whether he slept much during the night. Certainly he was up and about early enough the following morning.

"That's curious," I heard him remark, as he ran his eye hastily over the first page of the morning paper, "but I rather expected something of the sort. Read that in the first column, Tom."

The story that he indicated had all the marks of having been dropped into place at the last moment as the city edition went to press in the small hours of the night.

It was headed:

GIRL'S BODY FOUND IN THICKET

The despatch was from a little town in New Jersey, and, when I saw the date line, it at once suggested to me, as it had to Guy, that this was in the vicinity that must have been traversed in order to reach the point from which had come the report of the bloody car that had seemed to tally with the description of that which Warrington had lost. It read:

"Hidden in the underbrush, not ten feet from one of the most travelled automobile roads in this section of the state, the body of a murdered girl was discovered late yesterday afternoon by a gang of Italian labourers employed on an estate nearby."

"Suspicion was at first directed by the local authorities at the labourers, but the manner of the finding of the body renders it improbable. Most of them are housed in some rough shacks up the road toward Tuxedo and were able to prove themselves of good character. Indeed, the trampled condition of the thicket plainly indicates, according to the local coroner, that the girl was brought there, probably already dead, in an automobile which drew up off the road as far as possible. The body then must have been thrown where it would be screened from sight by the thick growth of trees and shrubbery.

"There was only one wound, in the chest. It is, however, a most peculiar wound, and shows that a terrific force must have been exerted in order to make it. A blow could hardly have accomplished it, so jagged were its edges, and if the girl had been struck by a passing high-speed car, as was at first suggested, there is no way to account for the entire lack of other wounds which must naturally have been inflicted by such an accident.

"Neither is the wound exactly like a pistol or gunshot wound, for, curiously enough, there was no mark showing the exit of a bullet, nor was any bullet found in the body after the most careful examination. The local authorities are completely mystified at the possible problems that may arise out of the case, especially as to the manner in which the unfortunate girl met her death."

"Until a late hour the body, which is of a girl perhaps twenty-three or four, of medium height, fair, good looking, and stylishly dressed, was still unidentified. She was unknown in this part of the country."

Almost before I had finished reading, Garrick had his hat and coat on and had shoved into his pocket a little detective camera.

"Strange about the bullet," I ruminated. "I wonder who she can be?"

Arthur B. Reeve

"Very strange," agreed Garrick, urging me on. "I think we ought to investigate the case."

As we hurried along to a restaurant for a bite of breakfast, he remarked, "The circumstances of the thing, coming so closely after the report about Warrington's car, are very suspicious—very. I feel sure that we shall find some connection between the two affairs."

Accordingly, we caught an early train and at the nearest railroad station to the town mentioned in the despatch engaged a hackman who knew the coroner, a local doctor.

The coroner was glad to assist us, though we were careful not to tell him too much of our own connection with the case. On the way over to the village undertaker's where the body had been moved, he volunteered the information that the New York police, whom he had notified immediately, had already sent a man up there, who had taken a description of the girl and finger prints, but had not, so far at least, succeeded in identifying the girl, at any rate on any of the lists of those reported missing.

"You see," remarked Garrick to me, "that is where the police have us at a disadvantage. They have organization on their side. A good many detectives make the mistake of antagonizing the police. But if you want results, that's fatal."

"Yes," I agreed, "it's impossible, just as it is to antagonize the newspapers."

"Exactly," returned Garrick. "My idea of the thing, Marshall, is that I should work with, not against, the regular detectives. They are all right, in fact indispensable. Half the secret of success nowadays is efficiency and organization. What I do believe is that organization plus science is what is necessary."

The local undertaking establishment was rather poorly equipped to take the place of a morgue and the authorities were making preparations to move the body to the nearest large city pending the disposal of the case. Local detectives had set to work, but so far had turned up nothing, not even the report which we had already received from McBirney regarding the blood-stained car that resembled Warrington's.

We arrived with the coroner fortunately just before the removal of the body to the city and by his courtesy were able to see it without any trouble.

Death, and especially violent death, are at best grewsome subjects, but when to that are added the sordid surroundings of a country undertaker's and the fact that the victim is a woman, it all becomes doubly tragic.

She was a rather flashily dressed girl, but remarkably good looking, in spite of the rouge and powder which had long since spoiled what might otherwise have been a clear and fine complexion. The roots of her hair showed plainly that it had been bleached.

Garrick examined the body closely, and more especially the jagged wound in the breast. I bent over also. It seemed utterly inexplicable. There was, he soon discovered, a sort of greasy, oleaginous deposit in the clotted blood of the huge cavity in the flesh. It interested him, and he studied it carefully for a long time, without saying a word.

"Some have said she was wounded by some kind of blunt instrument," put in the coroner. "Others that she was struck by a car. But it's my opinion that she was killed by a rifle bullet of some kind, although what could have become of the bullet is beyond me. I've probed for it, but it isn't there."

Garrick finished his minute examination of the wound without passing any comment on it of his own.

"Now, if you will be kind enough to take us around to the place where the body was discovered," he concluded, "I think we shall not trespass on your time further."

In his own car, the coroner drove us up the road in the direction of the New York state boundary to the spot where the body had been found. It was a fine, well-oiled road and I noticed the number and high quality of the cars which passed us.

When we arrived at the spot where the body of the unfortunate girl had been discovered, Garrick began a minute search. I do not think for a moment that he expected to find any weapon, or even the trace of one. It seemed hopeless also to attempt to pick out any of the footprints. The earth was soft and even muddy, but so many feet had trodden it down since the first alarm had been given that it would have been impossible to extricate one set of footprints from another, much less to tell whether any of them had been made by the perpetrators of the crime.

Still, there seemed to be something in the mud, just off the side of the road, that did interest Garrick. Very carefully, so as not to destroy anything himself which more careless searchers might have left, he began a minute study of the ground.

Apparently he was rewarded, for, although he said nothing, he took a hasty glance at the direction of the sun, up-ended the camera he had brought, and began to photograph the ground itself, or rather some curious marks on it which I could barely distinguish.

The coroner and I looked on without saying a word. He, at least, I am sure, thought that Garrick had suddenly taken leave of his senses.

That concluded Garrick's investigation, and, after thanking the coroner, who had gone out of his way to accommodate us, we started back to town.

"Well," I remarked, as we settled ourselves for the tedious ride into the city in the suburban train, "we don't seem to have added much to the sum of human knowledge by this trip."

"Oh, yes, we have," he returned, almost cheerfully, patting the black camera which he had folded and slipped into his pocket. "We'll just preserve the records which I have here. Did you notice what it was that I photographed?"

"I saw something," I replied, "but I couldn't tell you what it was."

"Well," he explained slowly as I opened my eyes wide in amazement at the minuteness of his researches, "those were the marks of the tire of an automobile that had been run up into the bushes from the road. You know every automobile tire leaves its own distinctive mark, its thumb print, as it were. When I have developed my films, you will see that the marks that have been left there are precisely like those left by the make of tires used on Warrington's car, according to the advertisement sent out by McBirney. Of course, that mere fact alone doesn't prove anything. Many cars may use that make of tires. Still, it is an interesting coincidence, and if the make had been different I should not feel half so encouraged about going ahead with this clew. We can't say anything definite, however, until I can compare the actual marks made by the tires on the stolen car with these marks which I have photographed and preserved."

If any one other than Garrick had conceived such a notion as the "thumb print" of an automobile tire, I might possibly have ventured to doubt it. As it was it gave food enough for thought to last the remainder of the journey back to town.

CHAPTER IV

THE LIQUID BULLET

On our return to the city, I was not surprised after our conversation over in New Jersey to find that Garrick had decided on visiting police headquarters. It was, of course, Commissioner Dillon, one of the deputies, whom he wanted to see. I had met Dillon myself some time before in connection with my study of the finger print system, and consequently needed no second introduction.

In his office on the second floor, the Commissioner greeted us cordially in his bluff and honest voice which both of us came to know and like so well later. Garrick had met him often and the cordiality of their relations was well testified to by Dillon's greeting.

"I thought you'd be here before long," he beamed on Garrick, as he led us into an inner sanctum. "Did you read in the papers this morning about that murder of a girl whose body was found up in New Jersey in the underbrush?"

"Not only that, but I've picked up a few things that your man overlooked," confided Garrick.

Dillon looked at him sharply for a moment. "Say," he said

Arthur B. Reeve

frankly, "that's one of the things I like about you, Garrick. You're on the job. Also, you're on the square. You don't go gumshoeing it around behind a fellow's back, and talking the same way. You play fair. Now, look here. Haven't I always played fair with you, Garrick?"

"Yes, Dillon," agreed Garrick, "you have always played fair. But what's the idea?"

"You came up here for information, didn't you?" persisted the commissioner.

Garrick nodded.

"Well do you know who that girl was who was murdered?" he asked leaning forward.

"No," admitted Garrick.

"Of course not," asserted Dillon triumphantly. "We haven't given it out yet—and I don't know as we shall."

"No," pursued Garrick, "I don't know and I'll admit that I'd like to know. My position is, as it always has been, that we shouldn't work at cross purposes. I have drawn my own conclusions on the case and, to put it bluntly, it seemed to me clear that she was of the demi-monde."

"She was—in a sense," vouchsafed the commissioner. "Now," he added, leaning forward impressively, "I'm going to tell you something. That girl—was one of the best stool pigeons we have ever had."

Both Garrick and I were listening intently at, the surprising revelation of the commissioner. He was pacing up and down, now, evidently much excited.

"As for me," he continued, "I hate the stool pigeon method as much as anyone can. I don't like it. I don't relish the idea of being in partnership with crooks in any degree. I hate an informer who worms himself or herself into a person's friendship for the purpose of betraying it. But the system is here. I didn't start it and I can't change it. As long as it's here I must accept it and do business under it. And, that being the case, I can't afford to let matters like this killing pass without getting revenge, swift and sure. You understand? Someone's going to suffer for the killing of that girl, not only because it was a brutal murder, but because the department has got to make an example or no one whom we employ is safe."

Dillon was shouldering his burly form up and down the office in his excitement. He paused in front of us, to proceed.

"I've got one of my best men on the case now—Inspector Herman. I'll introduce you to him, if he happens to be around. Herman's all right. But here you come in, Garrick, and tell me you picked up something that my man missed up there in Jersey. I know it's the truth, too. I've worked with you and seen enough of you to know that you wouldn't say a thing like that as a bluff to me."

Dillon was evidently debating something in his mind.

"Herman'll have to stand it," he went on, half to himself. "I don't care whether he gets jealous or not."

He paused and looked Garrick squarely in the eye, as he led up to his proposal. "Garrick," he said slowly, "I'd like to have you take up the case for us, too. I've heard already that you are working on the automobile cases. You see, I have ways of getting information myself. We're not so helpless as your friend McBirney, maybe, thinks."

He faced us and it was almost as if he read our minds.

"For instance," he proceeded, "it may interest you to know that we have just planned a new method to recover stolen automobiles and apprehend the thieves. A census of all cars in the questionable garages of the city has been taken, and each day every policeman is furnished with descriptions of cars stolen in the past twenty-four hours. The policeman then is supposed to inspect the garages in his district and if he finds a machine that shouldn't be there, according to the census, he sees to it that it isn't removed from the place until it is identified. The description of this Warrington car has gone out with extra special orders, and if it's in New York I think we'll find it."

"I think you'll find," remarked Garrick quietly, "that this machine of Warrington's isn't in the city, at all."

"I hardly think it is, myself," agreed Dillon. "Whoever it was who took it is probably posted about our new scheme. That's not the point I was driving at. You see, Garrick, our trails cross in these cases in a number of ways. Now, I have a little secret fund at my disposal. In so far as the affair involved the murder of that girl—and I'm convinced that it does—will you consider that you are working for the city, too? The whole thing dovetails. You don't have to neglect one client to serve another. I'll do anything I can to help you with the auto cases. In fact, you'll do better by both clients by joining the cases."

"Dillon," answered Garrick quickly, "you've always been on the level with me. I can trust you. Consider that it is a bargain. We'll work together. Now, who was the girl?"

"Her name was Rena Taylor," replied Dillon, apparently much gratified at the success of his proposal. "I had her at work getting evidence against a ladies' poolroom in Forty-seventh Street—an elusive place that we've never been able to 'get right.'"

Garrick shot a quick glance at me. Evidently we were on the right trail, anyhow.

"I don't know yet just what happened," continued Dillon, "but I do know that she had the goods on it. As nearly as I can find out, a stranger came to the place well introduced, a man, accompanied by a woman. They got into some of the games. The man seems to have excused himself. Apparently he found Rena Taylor alone in a room in some part of the house. No one heard a pistol shot, but then I think they would lie about that, all right."

Dillon paused. "The strange thing is, however," he resumed, "that we haven't been able to find in the house a particle of evidence that a murder or violence of any kind has been done. One fact is established, though, incontrovertibly. Rena Taylor disappeared from that gambling house the same night and about the same time that Warrington's car disappeared. Then we find her dead over in New Jersey."

"And I find reports and traces that the car has been in the vicinity," added Garrick.

"You see," beamed Dillon, "that's how we work together. Say you MUST meet Herman."

He rang a bell and a blue-coated man opened the door. "Call Herman, Jim," he said, then, as the man disappeared, he went on to us, "I have given Herman carte-blanche instructions to conduct a thorough investigation. He has been getting the goods on another swell joint on the next street, in Forty-eighth, a joint that is just feeding on young millionaires in this town, and is or will be the cause of more crime and broken hearts if I don't land it and break it up than any such place has been for years." The door opened, and Dillon said, "Herman, shake hands with Mr. Garrick and Mr. Marshall."

The detective was a quiet, gentlemanly sort of fellow who looked rugged and strong, a fighter to be respected. In fact I would much rather have had a man like him with us than against us. I knew Garrick's aversion to the regular detective and was not surprised that he did not overwhelm Mr. Herman by the cordiality of his greeting. Garrick always played a lone hand, preferred it and had taken Dillon into his confidence only because of his official position and authority.

"These gentlemen are going to work independently on that Rena Taylor case," explained Dillon. "I want you to give Mr. Garrick every assistance, Herman."

Garrick nodded with a show of cordiality and Herman replied in about the same spirit. I could not fancy our getting very much assistance from the regular detective force, with the exception of Dillon. And I noticed, also, that Garrick was not volunteering any information except what was necessary in good faith. Already I began to wonder how this peculiar bargain would turn out.

"Just who and what was Rena Taylor?" asked Garrick finally.

Inspector Herman shot a covert glance at Dillon before replying and the commissioner hastened to reassure him, "I have told Mr. Garrick that she was one of our best stool pigeons and had been working on the gambling cases."

Like all detectives on a case, Herman was averse to parting

with any information, and I felt that it was natural, for if he succeeded in working it out human nature was not such as to willingly share the glory.

"Oh," he replied airily, "she was a girl who had knocked about considerably in the Tenderloin. I don't know just what her story was, but I suppose there was some fellow who got her to come to New York and then left her in the lurch. She wasn't a New Yorker. She seems to have drifted from one thing to another—until finally in order to get money she came down and offered her services to the police, in this gambling war."

Herman had answered the question, but when I examined the answer I found it contained precious little. Perhaps it was indeed all he knew, for, although Garrick put several other questions to him and he answered quite readily and with apparent openness, there was very little more that we learned.

"Yes," concluded Herman, "someone cooked her, all right. They don't take long to square things with anyone who raps to the 'bulls.'"

"That's right," agreed Garrick. "And the underworld isn't alone in that feeling. No one likes a 'snitch.'"

"Bet your life," emphasized Herman heartily, then edging toward the door, he said, "Well, gentlemen, I'm glad to meet you and I'll work with you. I wish you success, all right. It's a hard case. Why, there wasn't any trace of a murder or violence in that place in which Rena Taylor must have been murdered. I suppose you have heard that there wasn't any bullet found in the body, either?"

"Yes," answered Garrick, "so far it does look inexplicable."

Inspector Herman withdrew. One could see that he had little faith in these "amateur" detectives.

A telephone message for Dillon about another departmental matter terminated our interview and we went our several ways.

"Much help I've ever got from a regular detective like Herman," remarked Garrick, phrasing my own idea of the matter, as we paid the fare of our cab a few minutes later and entered his office.

"Yes," I agreed. "Why, he's even stumped at the start by the mystery of there being no bullet. I'm glad you said nothing about the cartridge, although I can't see for the life of me what good it is to us."

I had ventured the remark, hoping to entice Garrick into talking. It worked, at least as far as Garrick wanted to talk yet.

"You'll see about the cartridge soon enough, Tom," he rejoined. "As for there being no bullet, there was a bullet— only it was of a kind you never dreamed of before."

He regarded me contemplatively for a moment, then leaned over and in a voice full of meaning, concluded, "That bullet was composed of something soft or liquid, probably confined in some kind of thin capsule. It mushroomed out like a dumdum bullet. It was deadly. But the chief advantage was that the heat that remained in Rena Taylor's body melted all evidence of the bullet. That was what caused that greasy, oleaginous appearance of the wound. The murderer thought he left no trail in the bullet in the corpse. In other words, it was practically a liquid bullet."

CHAPTER V

THE BLACKMAILER

It was late in the afternoon, while Garrick was still busy with a high-powered microscope, making innumerable micro-photographs, when the door of the office opened softly and a young lady entered.

As she advanced timidly to us, we could see that she was tall and gave promise of developing with years into a stately woman—a pronounced brunette, with sparkling black eyes. I had not met her before, yet somehow I could not escape the feeling that she was familiar to me.

It was not until she spoke that I realized that it was the eyes, not the face, which I recognized.

"You are Mr. Garrick?" she asked of Guy in a soft, purring voice which, I felt, masked a woman who would fight to the end for anyone or anything she really loved.

Then, before Guy could answer, she explained, "I am Miss Violet Winslow. A friend of mine, Mr. Warrington, has told me that you are investigating a peculiar case for him—the strange loss of his car."

Garrick hastened to place a chair for her in the least cluttered and dusty part of the room. There she sat, looking up at him earnestly, a dainty contrast to the den in which Garrick was working out the capture of criminals, violent and vicious.

"I have the honor to be able to say, 'Yes' to all that you have asked, Miss Winslow," he replied. "Is there any way in which I can be of service to you?"

I thought a smile played over his face at the thought that perhaps she might have come to ask him to work for three clients instead of two.

At any rate, the girl was very much excited and very much in earnest, as she opened her handbag and drew from it a letter which she handed to Garrick.

"I received that letter," she explained, speaking rapidly, "in the noon mail to-day. I don't know what to make of it. It worries me to get such a thing. What do you suppose it was sent to me for? Who could have sent it?"

She was leaning forward artlessly on her crossed knee looking expectantly up into Garrick's face, oblivious to everything else, even her own enticing beauty. There was something so simple and sincere about Violet Winslow that one felt instinctively that nothing was too great a price to shield her from the sordid and the evil in the world. Yet something had happened that had brought her already into the office of a detective.

Garrick had glanced quickly at the outside of the slit envelope. The postmark showed that it had been mailed early that morning at the general post office and that there was slight chance of tracing anything in that direction.

Then he opened it and read. The writing was in a bold scrawl and hastily executed:

You have heard, no doubt, of the alleged loss of an automobile by Mr. Mortimer Warrington. I have seen your name mentioned in the society columns of the newspapers in connection with him several times lately. Let a disinterested person whom you do not know warn you in time. There is more back of it than he will care to tell. I can say nothing of the nefarious uses to which that car has been put, but you will learn more shortly. Meanwhile, let me inform you that he and some of the wilder of his set had that night planned a visit to a gambling house on Forty-eighth Street. I myself saw the car standing before another gambling den on Forty-seventh Street about the same time. This place, I may as well inform you, bears an unsavory reputation as a gambling joint to which young ladies of the fastest character are admitted. If you will ask someone in whom you have confidence and whom you can ask to work secretly for you to look up the records, you will find that much of the property on these two blocks, and these two places in particular, belongs to the Warrington estate. Need I say more?

The letter was without superscription or date and was signed merely with the words, "A Well-Wisher." The innuendo of the thing was apparent.

"Of course," she remarked, as Garrick finished reading, and before he could speak, "I know there is something back of it. Some person is trying to injure Mortimer. Still—"

She did not finish the sentence. It was evident that the "well-wisher" need not have said more in order to sow the seeds of doubt.

As I watched her narrowly, I fancied also that from her tone

Arthur B. Reeve

the newspapers had not been wholly wrong in mentioning their names together recently.

"I hadn't intended to say anything more than to explain how I got the letter," she went on wistfully. "I thought that perhaps you might be interested in it."

She paused and studied the toe of her dainty boot. "And, of course," she murmured, "I know that Mr. Warrington isn't dependent for his income on the rent that comes in from such places. But—but I wish just the same that it wasn't true. I tried to call him up about the letter, but he wasn't at the office of the Warrington estate, and no one seemed to know just where he was."

She kept her eyes downcast as though afraid to betray just what she felt.

"You will leave this with me?" asked Garrick, still scrutinizing the letter.

"Certainly," she replied. "That is what I brought it for. I thought it was only fair that he should know about it."

Garrick regarded her keenly for a moment. "I am sure, Miss Winslow," he said, "that Mr. Warrington will thank you for your frankness. More than that, I feel sure that you need have no cause to worry about the insinuations of this letter. Don't judge harshly until you have heard his side. There's a good deal of graft and vice talk flying around loose these days. Miss Winslow, you may depend on me to dig the truth out and not deceive you."

"Thank you so much," she said, as she rose to go; then, in a burst of confidence, added, "Of course, after all, I don't care so much about it myself—but, you know, my aunt—is so dreadfully prim and proper that she couldn't forgive a thing like this. She'd never let Mr. Warrington call on me again."

Violet stopped and bit her lip. She had evidently not intended to say as much as that. But having once said it, she did not seem to wish to recall the words, either.

"There, now," she smiled, "don't you even hint to him that that was one of the reasons I called."

Garrick had risen and was standing beside her, looking down earnestly into her upturned face.

"I think I understand, Miss Winslow," he said in a low voice, rapidly. "I cannot tell you all—yet. But I can promise you that even if all were told—the truth, I mean—your faith in Warrington would be justified." He leaned over. "Trust me," he said simply.

As she placed her small hand in Garrick's, she looked up into his face, and with suppressed emotion, answered, "Thank you—I—I will."

Then, with a quick gathering of her skirts, she turned and almost fled from the room.

She had scarcely closed the door before Garrick was telephoning anxiously all over the city in order to get in touch with Warrington himself.

"I'm not going to tell him too much about her visit," he remarked, with a pleased smile at the outcome of the interview, though his face clouded as his eye fell again on the black-mailing letter, lying before him. "It might make him think too highly of himself. Besides, I want to see, too, whether he has told us the whole truth about the affair that night."

Somehow or other it seemed impossible to find Warrington in any of his usual haunts, either at his office or at his club.

Garrick had given it up, almost, as a bad job, when, half an hour later, Warrington himself burst in on us, apparently expecting more news about his car.

Instead, Garrick handed him the letter.

"Say," he demanded as he ran through it with puckered face, then slapped it down on the table before Guy, in a high state of excitement, "what do you make of that?"

He looked from one to the other of us blankly.

"Isn't it bad enough to lose a car without being slandered about it into the bargain?" he asked heatedly, then adding in disgust, "And to do it in such an underhand way, writing to a girl like Violet, and never giving me a chance to square myself. If I could get my hands on that fellow," he added viciously, "I'd qualify him for the coroner!"

Warrington had flown into a towering and quite justifiable rage. Garrick, however, ignored his anger as natural under the circumstances, and was about to ask him a question.

"Just a moment, Garrick," forestalled Warrington. "I know just what you are going to say. You are going to ask me about those gambling places. Now, Garrick, I give you my word of honor that I did not know until to-day that the property in that neighborhood was owned by our estate. I have been in that joint on Forty-eighth Street—I'll admit that. But, you know, I'm no gambler. I've gone simply to see the life, and—well, it has no attraction for me. Racing cars and motorboats don't go with poker chips and the red and black—not with me. As for the other place, I don't know any more about it than—than you do," he concluded vehemently.

Warrington faced Garrick, his steel-blue eye unwavering. "You see, it's like this," he resumed passionately, "since this vice investigation began, I have read a lot about landlords. Then, too," he interjected with a mock wry face, "I knew that Violet's Aunt Emma had been a crusader or something of the sort. You see, virtue is NOT its own reward. I don't get credit even for what I intended to do—quite the contrary."

"How's that?" asked Garrick, respecting the young man's temper.

"Why, it just occurred to me lately to go scouting around the city, looking at the Warrington holdings, making some personal inquiries as to the conditions of the leases, the character of the tenants, and the uses to which they put the properties. The police have compiled a list of all the questionable places in the city and I have compared it with the list of our properties. I hadn't come to this one yet. But I shall call up our agent, make him admit it, and cancel that lease. I'll close 'em up. I'll fight until every—"

"No," interrupted Garrick, quickly, "no—not yet. Don't make any move yet. I want to find out what the game is. It may be that it is someone who has tried and failed to get your tenant to come across with graft money. If we act without finding out first, we might be playing into the hands of this blackmailer."

Garrick had been holding the letter in his hand, examining it critically. While he was speaking, he had taken a toothpick and was running it hastily over the words, carefully studying them. His face was wrinkled, as if he were in deep thought.

Without saying anything more, Garrick walked over to the

Arthur B. Reeve

windows and pulled down the dark shades. Then he unrolled a huge white sheet at one end of the office.

From a corner he drew out what looked like a flat-topped stand, about the height of his waist, with a curious box-like arrangement on it, in which was a powerful light. For several minutes, he occupied himself with the adjustment of this machine, switching the light off and on and focussing the lenses.

Then he took the letter to Miss Winslow, laid it flat on the machine, switched on the light and immediately on the sheet appeared a very enlarged copy of the writing.

"This is what has been called a rayograph by a detective of my acquaintance," explained Garrick. "In some ways it is much superior to using a microscope."

He was tracing over the words with a pointer, much as he had already done with the toothpick.

"Now, you must know," he continued, "or you may not know, but it is a well-proved fact, that those who suffer from various affections of the nerves or heart often betray the fact in their handwriting. Of course, in cases where the disease has progressed very far it may be evident to the naked eye even in the ordinary handwriting. But, it is there, to the eye of the expert, even in incipient cases.

"In short," he continued, engrossed in his subject, "what really happens is that the pen acts as a sort of sphygmograph, registering the pulsations. I think you can readily see that when the writing is thrown on a screen, enlarged by the rayograph, the tremors of the pen are quite apparent."

I studied the writing, following his pointer as it went over the lines and I began to understand vaguely what he was driving at.

"The writer of that blackmailing letter," continued Garrick, "as I have discovered both by hastily running over it with a tooth-pick and, more accurately, by enlarging and studying it with the rayograph, is suffering from a peculiar conjunction of nervous trouble and disease of the heart which is latent and has not yet manifested itself, even to him."

Garrick studied the writing, then added, thoughtfully, "if I knew him, I might warn him in time."

"A fellow like that needs only the warning of a club or of a good pair of fists," growled Warrington, impatiently. "How are you going to work to find him?"

"Well," reasoned Garrick, rolling up the sheet and restoring the room to its usual condition, "for one thing, the letter makes it pretty evident that he knows something about the gambling joint, perhaps is one of the regular habitues of the place. That was why I didn't want you to take any steps to close up the place immediately. I want to go there and look it over while it is in operation. Now, you admit that you have been in the place, don't you?"

"Oh, yes," he replied, "I've been there with Forbes and the other fellows, but as I told you, I don't go in for that sort of thing."

"Well," persisted Garrick, "you are sufficiently known, any way, to get in again."

"Certainly. I can get in again. The man at the door will let me in—and a couple of friends, too, if that's what you mean."

"That is exactly what I mean," returned Garrick. "It's no use to go early. I want to see the place in full blast, just as the after-theatre crowd is coming in. Suppose you meet us, Warrington, about half past ten or so. We can get in. They don't know anything yet about your intention to cancel the lease and close up the place, although apparently someone suspects it, or he wouldn't have been so anxious to get that letter off to Miss Winslow."

"Very well," agreed Warrington, "I will meet you at the north end of 'Crime Square,' as you call it, at that time. Good luck until then."

"Not a bad fellow, at all," commented Garrick when Warrington had disappeared down the hall from the office. "I believe he means to do the square thing by every one. It's a shame he has been dragged into a mess like this, that may affect him in ways that he doesn't suspect. Oh, well, there is nothing we can do for the present. I'll just add this clew of the handwriting to the clew of the automobile tires against the day when we get—pshaw!—he has taken the letter with him. I suppose it is safe enough in his possession, though. He can't wait until he has proved to Violet that he is honest. I don't blame him much. I told you, you know, that the younger set are just crazy over Violet Winslow."

CHAPTER VI

THE GAMBLING DEN

In spite of the agitation that was going on at the time in the city against gambling, we had no trouble in being admitted to the place in Forty-eighth Street. They seemed to recognise Warrington, for no sooner had the lookout at the door peered through a little grating and seen him than the light woodwork affair was opened.

To me, with even my slender knowledge of such matters, it had seemed rather remarkable that only such a door should guard a place that was so notorious. Once inside, however, the reason was apparent. It didn't. On the outside there was merely such a door as not to distinguish the house, a three-story and basement dwelling, of old brownstone, from the others in the street.

As the outside door shut quickly, we found ourselves in a sort of vestibule confronted by another door. Between the two the lookout had his station.

The second door was of the "ice-box" variety, as it was popularly called at the time, of heavy oak, studded with ax-defying bolts, swung on delicately balanced and oiled hinges, carefully concealed, about as impregnable as a door of steel might be.

There were, as we found later, some steel doors inside, leading to the roof and cellar, though not so thick. The windows were carefully guarded inside by immense steel bars. The approaches from the back were covered with a steel network and every staircase was guarded by a collapsible door. There seemed to be no point of attack that had been left unguarded.

Yet, unless one had been like ourselves looking for these fortifications, they would not have appeared much in evidence in the face of the wealth of artistic furnishings that was lavished on every hand. Inside the great entrance door was a sort of marble reception hall, richly furnished, and giving anything but the impression of a gambling house. As a matter of fact, the first floor was pretty much of a blind. The gambling was all upstairs.

We turned to a beautiful staircase of carved wood, and ascended. Everywhere were thick rugs into which the feet sank almost ankle deep. On the walls were pictures that must have cost a small fortune. The furniture was of the costliest; there were splendid bronzes and objects of art on every hand.

Gambling was going on in several rooms that we passed, but the main room was on the second floor, a large room reconstructed in the old house, with a lofty ceiling and exquisitely carved trim. Concealed in huge vases were the lights, a new system, then, which shed its rays in every direction without seeming to cast a shadow anywhere. The room was apparently windowless, and yet, though everyone was smoking furiously, the ventilation must have been perfect.

There was, apparently, a full-fledged poolroom in one part of the house, closed now, of course, as the races for the day were run. But I could imagine it doing a fine business in the afternoon. There were many other games now in progress, games of every description, from poker to faro, keno, klondike, and roulette. There was nothing of either high or low degree with which the venturesome might not be accommodated.

As Warrington conducted us from one room to another, Garrick noted each carefully. Along the middle of the large room stretched a roulette table. We stopped to watch it.

"Crooked as it can be," was Garrick's comment after watching it for five minutes or so.

He had not said it aloud, naturally, for even the crowd in evening clothes about it, who had lost or would lose, would have resented such an imputation.

For the most part there was a solemn quiet about the board, broken only by the rattle of the ball and the click of chips. There was an absence of the clink of gold pieces that one hears as the croupier rakes them in at the casinos on the continent. Nor did there seem to be the tense faces that one might expect. Often there was the glint of an eye, or a quick and muffled curse, but for the most part everyone, no matter how great a loser, seemed respectable and prosperous. The tragedies, as we came to know, were elsewhere.

We sauntered into another room where they were playing keno. Keno was, we soon found, a development or an outgrowth of lotto, in which cards were sold to the players, bearing numbers which were covered with buttons, as in lotto. The game was won when a row was full after drawing forth the numbers on little balls from a "goose."

"Like the roulette wheel," said Garrick grimly, "the 'goose' is crooked, and if I had time I could show you how it is done."

We passed by the hazard boards as too complicated for the limited time at our disposal.

It was, however, the roulette table which seemed to interest Garrick most, partly for the reason that most of the players flocked about it.

The crowd around the table on the second floor was several deep, now. Among those who were playing I noticed a new face. It was of a tall, young man much the worse, apparently, for the supposed good time he had had already. The game seemed to have sobered him up a bit, for he was keen as to mind, now, although a trifle shaky as to legs.

He glanced up momentarily from his close following of the play as we approached.

"Hello, W.," he remarked, as he caught sight of our young companion.

A moment later he had gone back to the game as keen as ever.

"Hello, F.," greeted Warrington. Then, aside to us, he added, "You know they don't use names now in gambling places if they can help it. Initials do just as well. That is Forbes, of whom I told you. He's a young fellow of good family—but I am afraid he is going pretty much to the bad, or will go, if he doesn't quit soon. I wish I could stop him. He's a nice chap. I knew him well at college and we have chummed about a great deal. He's here too much of the time for his own good."

The thing was fascinating, I must admit, no matter what the

morals of it were. I became so engrossed that I did not notice a man standing opposite us. I was surprised when he edged over towards us slowly, then whispered to Garrick, "Meet me downstairs in the grill in five minutes, and have a bite to eat. I have something important to say. Only, be careful and don't get me 'in Dutch' here."

The man had a sort of familiar look and his slang certainly reminded me of someone we had met.

"Who was it?" I inquired under my breath, as he disappeared among the players.

"Didn't you recognize him?" queried Garrick. "Why, that was Herman, Dillon's man,—the fellow, you know, who is investigating this place."

I had not recognized the detective in evening clothes. Indeed, I felt that unless he were known here already his disguise was perfect.

Garrick managed to leave Warrington for a time under the pretext that he wanted him to keep an eye on Forbes while we explored the place further. We walked leisurely down the handsome staircase into the grill and luncheon room downstairs.

"Well, have you found out anything?" asked a voice behind us.

We turned. It was Herman who had joined us. Without pausing for an answer he added, "I suppose you are aware of the character of this place? It looks fine, but the games are all crooked, and I guess there are some pretty desperate characters here, from all accounts. I shouldn't like to fall afoul of any of them, if I were you."

"Oh, no," replied Garrick, "it wouldn't be pleasant. But we came in well introduced, and I don't believe anyone suspects."

Several others, talking and laughing loudly to cover their chagrin over losses, perhaps, entered the buffet.

With the gratuitous promise to stand by us in trouble of any kind, Herman excused himself, and returned to watch the play about the roulette table.

Garrick and I leisurely finished the little bite of salad we had ordered, then strolled upstairs again.

The play was becoming more and more furious. Forbes was losing again, but was sticking to it with a grim determination that was worthy of a better cause. Warrington had already made one attempt to get him away but had not succeeded.

"Well," remarked Garrick, as we three made our way slowly to the coatroom downstairs, "I think we have seen enough of this for to-night. It isn't so very late, after all. I wonder if it would be possible to get into that ladies' poolroom on the next street? I should like to see that place."

"Angus could get us in, if anyone could," replied Warrington thoughtfully. "Wait here a minute. I'll see if I can get him away from the wheel long enough."

Five minutes later he came back, with Forbes in tow. He shook hands with us cordially, in fact a little effusively. Perhaps I might have liked the young fellow if I could have taken him in hand for a month or two, and knocked some of the silly ideas he had out of his head.

Forbes called a taxicab, a taxicab apparently being the open sesame. One might have gone afoot and have looked ever so much like a "good thing" and he would not have been admitted. But such is the simplicity of the sophistication of the keepers of such places that a motor car opens all locks and bolts.

It seemed to be a peculiar place and as nearly as I could make out was in a house almost in the rear of the one we had just come from.

We were politely admitted by a negro maid, who offered to take our coats.

"No," answered Forbes, apparently with an eye to getting out as quickly as possible, "we won't stay long tonight. I just came around to introduce my friends to Miss Lottie. I must get back right away."

For some reason or other he seemed very anxious to leave us. I surmised that the gambling fever was running high and that he had hopes of a change of luck. At any rate, he was gone, and we had obtained admittance to the ladies' pool room.

We strolled into one of the rooms in which the play was on. The game was at its height, with huge stacks of chips upon the tables and the players chatting gayly. There was no large crowd there, however. Indeed, as we found afterward, it was really in the afternoon that it was most crowded, for it was rather a poolroom than a gambling joint, although we gathered from the gossip that some stiff games of bridge were played there. Both men and women were seated at the poker game that was in progress before the little green table. The women were richly attired and looked as if they had come from good families.

We were introduced to several, but as it was evident that they were passing under assumed names, whatever the proprietor of the place might know of them, I made little effort to remember the names, although I did study the faces carefully.

It was not many minutes before we met Miss Lottie, as everyone called the woman who presided over this feminine realm of chance. Miss Lottie was a finely gowned woman, past middle age, but remarkably well preserved, and with a figure that must have occasioned much thought to fashion along the lines of the present slim styles. There seemed to be a man who assisted in the conduct of the place, a heavy-set fellow with a closely curling mustache. But as he kept discreetly in the offing, we did not see much of him.

Miss Lottie was frankly glad to see us, coming so well introduced, and outspokenly disappointed that we would not take a seat in the game that was in progress. However, Garrick passed that over by promising to come around soon. Excise laws were apparently held in puny respect in this luxurious atmosphere, and while the hospitable Miss Lottie went to summon a servant to bring refreshments—at our expense—we had ample opportunity to glance about at the large room in which we were seated.

Garrick gazed long and curiously at an arc-light enclosed in a soft glass globe in the center of the ceiling, as though it had suggested an idea of some sort to him.

Miss Lottie, who had left us for a few moments, returned unexpectedly to find him still gazing at it.

"We keep that light burning all the time," she remarked, noticing his gaze. "You see, in the daytime we never use the windows. It is always just like it is now, night or day. It makes no difference with us. You know, if we ever should be disturbed by the police," she rattled on, "this is my house and I am giving a little private party to a number of my friends."

I had heard of such places but had never seen one before. I knew that well-dressed women, once having been caught in the toils of gambling, and perhaps afraid to admit their losses to their husbands, or, often having been introduced through gambling to far worse evils, were sent out from these poker rendezvous to the Broadway cafes, there to flirt with men, and rope them into the game.

I could not help feeling that perhaps some of the richly gowned women in the house were in reality "cappers" for the game. As I studied the faces, I wondered what tragedies lay back of these rouged and painted faces. I saw broken homes, ruined lives, even lost honor written on them. Surely, I felt, this was a case worth taking up if by any chance we could put a stop or even set a limitation to this nefarious traffic.

"Have you ever had any trouble?" Garrick asked as we sipped at the refreshments.

"Very little," replied Miss Lottie, then as if the very manner of our introduction had stamped us all as "good fellows" to whom she could afford to be a little confidential in capturing our patronage, she added nonchalantly, "We had a sort of wild time a couple of nights ago."

"How was that?" asked Garrick in a voice of studied politeness that carefully concealed the aching curiosity he had for her to talk.

"Well," she answered slowly, "several ladies and gentlemen were here, playing a little high. They—well, they had a little too much to drink, I guess. There was one girl, who was the worst of all. She was pretty far gone. Why, we had to put her out—carry her out to the car that she had come in with her friend. You know we can't stand for any rough stuff like that—no sir. This house is perfectly respectable and proper and our patrons understand it."

The story, or rather, the version of it, seemed to interest Garrick, as I knew it would.

"Who was the girl?" he asked casually. "Did you know her? Was she one of your regular patrons?"

"Knew her only by sight," returned Miss Lottie hastily, now a little vexed, I imagined, at Guy's persistence, "like lots of people who are introduced here—and come again several times."

The woman was evidently sorry that she had mentioned the incident, and was trying to turn the conversation to the advantages of her establishment, not the least of which were her facilities for private games in little rooms in various parts of the house. It seemed all very risque to me, although I tried to appear to think it quite the usual thing, though I was careful to say that hers was the finest of such places I had ever seen. Still, the memory of Garrick's questioning seemed to linger. She had not expected, I knew, that we would take any further interest in her story than to accept it as proof of how careful she was of her clientele.

Garrick was quick to take the cue. He did not arouse any further suspicion by pursuing the subject. Apparently he was convinced that it had been Rena Taylor of whom Miss Lottie spoke. What really happened we knew no more now than before. Perhaps Miss Lottie herself knew—or she might not know. Garrick quite evidently was willing to let future developments in the case show what had really happened.

There was nothing to be gained by forcing things at this stage of the game, either in the gambling den around the corner or here.

We chatted along for several minutes longer on inconsequential subjects, treating as important those trivialities which Bohemia considers important and scoffing at the really good and true things of life that the demi-monde despises. It was all banality now, for we had touched upon the real question in our minds and had bounded as lightly off it as a toy balloon bounds off an opposing surface.

Warrington had kept silent during the visit, I noticed, and seemed relieved when it was over. I could not imagine that he was known here inasmuch as they treated him quite as they treated us.

Apparently, though, he had no relish for a possible report of the excursion to get to Miss Winslow's ears. He was the first to leave, as Garrick, after paying for our refreshments and making a neat remark or two about the tasteful way in which the gambling room was furnished, rescued our hats and coats from the negro servant, and said good-night with a promise to drop in again.

"What would Mrs. de Lancey think of THAT?" Garrick could not help saying, as we reached the street.

Warrington gave a nervous little forced laugh, not at all such as he might have given had Mrs. de Lancey not been the aunt of the girl who had entered his life.

Then he caught himself and said hastily, "I don't care what she thinks. It's none of her—"

He cut the words short, as if fearing to be misinterpreted

either way.

For several squares he plodded along silently, then, as we had accomplished the object of the evening, excused himself, with the request that we keep him fully informed of every incident in the case.

"Warrington doesn't wear his heart on his sleeve," commented Garrick as we bent our steps to our own, or rather his, apartment, "but it is evident enough that he is thinking all the time of Violet Winslow."

CHAPTER VII

THE MOTOR BANDIT

Early the next morning, the telephone bell began to ring violently. The message must have been short, for I could not gather from Garrick's reply what it was about, although I could tell by the startled look on his face that something unexpected had happened.

"Hurry and finish dressing, Tom," he called, as he hung up the receiver.

"What's the matter?" I asked, from my room, still struggling with my tie.

"Warrington was severely injured in a motor-car accident late last night, or rather early this morning, near Tuxedo."

"Near Tuxedo?" I repeated incredulously. "How could he have got up there? It was midnight when we left him in New York."

"I know it. Apparently he must have wanted to see Miss Winslow. She is up there, you know. I suppose that in order to be there this morning, early, he decided to start after he left us. I thought he seemed anxious to get away. Besides, you remember he took that letter yesterday afternoon, and I totally forgot to ask him for it last night. I'll wager it was on account of that slanderous letter that he wanted to go, that he wanted to explain it to her as soon as he could."

There had been no details in the hasty message over the wire, except that Warrington was now at the home of a Doctor Mead, a local physician in a little town across the border of New York and New Jersey. The more I thought about it, the more I felt that it was extremely unlikely that it could have been an accident, after all. Might it not have been the result of an attack or a trap laid by some strong-arm man who had set out to get him and had almost succeeded in accomplishing his purpose of "getting him right," to use the vernacular of the class?

We made the trip by railroad, passing the town where the report had come to us before of the finding of the body of Rena Taylor. There was, of course, no one at the station to meet us, and, after wasting some time in learning the direction, we at last walked to Dr. Mead's cottage, a quaint home, facing the state road that led from Suffern up to the Park, and northward.

Dr. Mead, who had telephoned, admitted us himself. We found Warrington swathed in bandages, and only half conscious. He had been under the influence of some drug, but, before that, the doctor told us, he had been unconscious and had only one or two intervals in which he was sufficiently lucid to talk.

"How did it happen?" asked Garrick, almost as soon as we had entered the doctor's little office.

"I had had a bad case up the road," replied the doctor slowly, "and it had kept me out late. I was driving my car along at a cautious pace homeward, some time near two o'clock, when I came to a point in the road where there are hills on one side and the river on the other. As I neared the curve, a rather sharp curve, too, I remember the lights on my own car were shining on the white fence that edged the river side of the road. I was keeping carefully on my own side, which was toward the hill.

"As I was about to turn, I heard the loud purring of an engine coming in my direction, and a moment later I saw a car with glaring headlights, driven at a furious pace, coming right at me. It slowed up a little, and I hugged the hill as close as I could, for I know some of these reckless young drivers up that way, and this curve was in the direction where the temptation is for one going north to get on the wrong side of the road—that is, my side—in order to take advantage of the natural slope of the macadam in turning the curve at high speed. Still, this fellow didn't prove so bad, after all. He gave me a wide berth.

"Just then there came a blinding flash right out of the darkness. Back of his car a huge, dark object had loomed up almost like a ghost. It was another car, back of the first one, without a single light, travelling apparently by the light shed by the forward car. It had overtaken the first and had cut in between us with not half a foot to spare on either side. It was the veriest piece of sheer luck I ever saw that we did not all go down together.

"With the flash I heard what sounded like a bullet zip out of the darkness. The driver of the forward car stiffened out for a moment. Then he pitched forward, helpless, over the steering wheel. His car dashed ahead, straight into the fence instead of taking the curve, and threw the unconscious driver. Then the car wrecked itself."

"And the car in the rear?" inquired Garrick eagerly.

"Dashed ahead between us safely around the curve—and was gone. I caught just one glimpse of its driver—a man all huddled up, his collar up over his neck and chin, his cap pulled forward over his eyes, goggles covering the rest of his face, and shrouded in what seemed to be a black coat, absolutely as unrecognizable as if he had been a phantom bandit, or death itself. He was steering with one hand, and in the other he held what must have been a revolver."

"And then?" prompted Garrick.

"I had stopped with my heart in my mouth at the narrowness of my own escape from the rushing black death. Pursuit was impossible. My car was capable of no such burst of speed as his. And then, too, there was a groaning man down in the ravine below. I got out, clambered over the fence, and down in the shrubbery into the pitch darkness.

"Fortunately, the man had been catapulted out before his car turned over. I found him, and with all the strength I could muster and as gently as I was able carried him up to the road. When I held him under the light of my lamps, I saw at once that there was not a moment to lose. I fixed him in the rear of my car as comfortably as I could and then began a race to get him home here where I have almost a private hospital of my own, as quickly as possible."

Cards in his pocket had identified Warrington and Dr. Mead remembered having heard the name. The prompt attention of the doctor had undoubtedly saved the young man's life.

Over and over again, Dr. Mead said, in his delirium Warrington had repeated the name, "Violet—Violet!" It was as Garrick had surmised, his desire to stand well in her eyes that had prompted the midnight journey. Yet who the assailant might be, neither Dr. Mead nor the broken raving of Warrington seemed to afford even the slightest clew. That he was a desperate character, without doubt in desperate straits over something, required no great acumen to deduce.

Toward morning in a fleeting moment of lucidity, Warrington had mentioned Garrick's name in such a way that Dr. Mead had looked it up in the telephone directory and then at the earliest moment had called up.

"Exactly the right thing," reassured Garrick. "Can't you think of anything else that would identify the driver of that other car?"

"Only that he was a wonderful driver, that fellow," pursued the doctor, admiration getting the better of his horror now that the thing was over. "I couldn't describe the car, except that it was a big one and seemed to be of a foreign make. He was crowding Warrington as much as he dared with safety to himself—and not a light on his own car, too, remember."

Garrick's face was puckered in thought.

"And the most remarkable thing of all about it," added the doctor, rising and going over to a white enameled cabinet in the corner of his office, "was that wound from the pistol."

The doctor paused to emphasize the point he was about to make. "Apparently it put Warrington out," he resumed. "And yet, after all, I find that it is only a very superficial flesh wound of the shoulder. Warrington's condition is really due to the contusions he received owing to his being thrown from the car. His car wasn't going very fast at the time, for it had slowed down for me. In one way that was fortunate— although one might say it was the cause of everything, since his slowing down gave the car behind a chance to creep up on him the few feet necessary.

"Really I am sure that even the shock of such a wound wasn't enough to make an experienced driver like Warrington lose control of the machine. It is a fairly wide curve, after all, and —well, my contention is proved by the fact that I examined the wreck of the car this morning and found that he had had time to shut off the gas and cut out the engine. He had time to think of and do that before he lost absolute control of the car."

Dr. Mead had been standing by the cabinet as he talked. Now he opened it and took from it the bullet which he had probed out of the wound. He looked at it a minute himself, then handed it to Garrick. I bent over also and examined it as it lay in Guy's hand.

At first I thought it was an ordinary bullet. But the more I examined it the more I was convinced that there was something peculiar about it. In the nose, which was steel-jacketed, were several little round depressions, just the least fraction of an inch in depth.

"It is no wonder Warrington was put out, even by that superficial wound," remarked Garrick at last. "His assailant's aim may have been bad, as it must necessarily have been from one rapidly approaching car at a person in another rapidly moving car, also. But the motor bandit, whoever he is, provided against that. That bullet is what is known as an anesthetic bullet."

"An anesthetic bullet?" repeated both Dr. Mead and myself. "What is that?"

"A narcotic bullet," Garrick explained, "a sleep-producing

bullet, if you please, a sedative bullet that lulls its victim into almost instant slumber. It was invented quite recently by a Pittsburgh scientist. The anesthetic bullet provides the poor marksman with all the advantages of the expert gunman of unerring aim."

I marvelled at the ingenuity of the man who could figure out how to overcome the seeming impossibility of accurate shooting from a car racing at high speed. Surely, he must be a desperate fellow.

While we were talking, the doctor's wife who had been attending Warrington until a nurse arrived, came to inform him that the effect of the sedative, which he had administered while Warrington was restless and groaning, was wearing off. We waited a little while, and then Dr. Mead himself informed us that we might see our friend for a minute.

Even in his half-drowsy state of pain Warrington appeared to recognise Garrick and assume that he had come in response to his own summons. Garrick bent down, and I could just distinguish what Warrington was trying to say to him.

"Wh—where's Violet?" he whispered huskily, "Does she know? Don't let her get—frightened—I'll be—all right."

Garrick laid his hand on Warrington's unbandaged shoulder, but said nothing.

"The—the letter," he murmured ramblingly. "I have it—in my apartment—in the little safe. I was going to Tuxedo—to see Violet—explain slander—tell her closing place—didn't know it was mine before. Good thing to close it—Forbes is a heavy loser. She doesn't know that."

Warrington lapsed back on his pillow and Dr. Mead beckoned

to us to withdraw without exciting him any further.

"What difference does it make whether she knows about Forbes or not?" I queried as we tiptoed down the hall.

Garrick shook his head doubtfully. "Can't say," he replied succinctly. "It may be that Forbes, too, has aspirations."

The idea sent me off into a maze of speculations, but it did not enlighten me much. At any rate, I felt, Warrington had said enough to explain his presence in that part of the country. On one thing, as I have said, Garrick had guessed right. The blackmailing letter and what we had seen the night before at the crooked gambling joint had been too much for him. He had not been able to rest as long as he was under a cloud with Miss Winslow until he had had a chance to set himself right in her eyes.

There seemed to be nothing that we could do for him just then. He was in excellent hands, and now that the doctor knew who he was, a trained nurse had even been sent for from the city and arrived on the train following our own, thus relieving Mrs. Mead of her faithful care of him.

Garrick gave the nurse strict instructions to make exact notes of anything that Warrington might say, and then requested the doctor to take us to the scene of the tragedy. We were about to start, when Garrick excused himself and hurried back into the house, reappearing in a few minutes.

"I thought perhaps, after all, it would be best to let Miss Winslow know of the accident, as long as it isn't likely to turn out seriously in the end for Warrington," he explained, joining us again in Dr. Mead's car which was waiting in front of the house. "So I called up her aunt's at Tuxedo and when Miss Winslow answered the telephone I broke the news to her as gently as I could. Warrington need have no fear about that girl," he added.

The wrecked car, we found, had not yet been moved, nor had the broken fence been repaired. It was, in fact, an accident worth studying topographically. That part of the road itself near the fence seemed to interest Garrick greatly. Two or three cars passed while we waited and he noted how carefully each of them seemed to avoid that side toward the broken fence, as though it were haunted.

"I hope they've all done that," Garrick remarked, as he continued to examine the road, which was a trifle damp under the high trees that shaded it.

As he worked, I could not believe that it was wholly fancy that caused me to think of him as searching with dilated nostrils, like a scientific human bloodhound. For, it was not long before I began to realize what he was looking for in the marks of cars left on the oiled roadway.

During perhaps half an hour he continued studying the road, above and below the exact point of the accident. At length a low exclamation from him brought me to his side. He had dropped down in the grease, regardless of his knees and was peering at some rather deep imprints in the surface dressing. There, for a few feet, were plainly the marks of the outside tires of a car, still unobliterated.

Garrick had pulled out copies of the photographs he had made of the tire marks that had been left at the scene of the finding of the unfortunate Rena Taylor's body, and was busy comparing them with the marks that were before him.

"Of course," Garrick muttered to me, "if the anti-skid marks of the tires were different, it would have proved nothing, just as in the other case where we looked for the tire prints. But here, too, a glance shows that at least it is the same make of tires."

He continued his comparison. It did not take me long to surmise what he was doing. He was taking the two sets of marks and, inch by inch, going over them, checking up the little round metal insertions that were placed in this style of tire to give it a firmer grip.

"Here's one missing, there's another," he cried excitedly. "By Jove, it can't be mere coincidence. There's one that is worn—another broken. They correspond. Yes, that MUST be the same car, in each case. And if it was the stolen car, then it was Warrington's own car that was used in pursuing him and in almost making away with him!"

CHAPTER VIII

THE EXPLANATION

We had not noticed a car which had stopped just past us and Garrick was surprised at hearing his own name called.

We looked up from contemplating the discovery he had made in the road, to see Miss Winslow waving to us. She had motored down from Tuxedo immediately after receiving the message over the telephone, and with her keen eye had picked out both the place of the accident and ourselves studying it.

As we approached, I could see that she was much more pale than usual. Evidently her anxiety for Warrington was thoroughly genuine. The slanderous letter had not shaken her faith in him, yet.

She had left her car and was walking back along the road with us toward the broken fence. Garrick had been talking to her earnestly and now, having introduced her to Dr. Mead, the doctor and he decided to climb down to inspect the wrecked car itself in the ravine below.

Miss Winslow cast a quick look from the broken fence down at the torn and twisted wreckage of the car and gave a suppressed little cry and shudder.

"How is Mortimer?" she asked of me eagerly, for I had agreed to stay with her while the others went down the slope. "I mean how is he really? Is he likely to be better soon, as Mr. Garrick said over the telephone?" she appealed.

"Surely—absolutely," I assured her, knowing that if Garrick had said that he had meant it. "Miss Winslow, believe me, neither Mr. Garrick nor Dr. Mead is concealing anything. It is pretty bad, of course. Such things are always bad. But it might be far worse. And besides, the worst now has passed."

Garrick had already promised to accompany her over to Dr. Mead's after he had made his examination of the wrecked car to confirm what the doctor had already observed. It took several minutes for them to satisfy themselves and meanwhile Violet Winslow, already highly unstrung by the news from Garrick, waited more and more nervously.

In spite of his careful examination of the wrecked car, Garrick found practically nothing more than Dr. Mead had already told him. It was with considerable relief that Miss Winslow saw the two again climbing up the slope in the direction of the road.

A few minutes later we were on our way back, Dr. Mead and Garrick leading the way in the doctor's car, while I accompanied Miss Winslow in her own car.

She said little, and it was plain to see that she was consumed by anxiety. Now and then she would ask a question about the accident, and although I tried in every way to divert her mind to other subjects she unfailingly came back to that.

Tempering the details as much as I could I repeated for her

just what had happened to the best of our knowledge.

"And you have no idea who it could have been?" she asked turning those liquid eyes of hers on my face.

If there were any secret about it, it was perhaps fortunate that I did not know. I don't think I am more than ordinarily susceptible and I know I did not delude myself that Miss Winslow ever could be anything except a friend to either Garrick or myself. But I felt I could not resist the appeal in those eyes. I wondered if even they, by some magic intuition, might not pierce the very soul of man and uncover a lying heart. I felt that Warrington could not have been other than he said he was and still have been hastening to meet those eyes.

"Miss Winslow," I answered, "I have no more idea than you have who it could be."

I was telling the truth and I felt that I could meet her gaze.

There must have been something about how I had phrased my answer that caused her to look at me more searchingly than before. Suddenly she turned her face away and gazed at the passing landscape from the car.

She said nothing, but as I continued to watch her finely moulded features, I saw that she was making an effort to control herself. It flashed over me, somehow, that perhaps, after all, she herself suspected someone. It was not that she said anything. It was merely an indefinable impression I received.

Had Warrington any enemies, not in the underworld, but among those of his own set, rivals, perhaps, who might even stoop to secure the aid of those of the underworld who could be bought to commit any crime in the calendar for a price? I did not pause to examine the plausibility or the impossibility of such a theory. What interested me was whether in her mind there was such a thought. Had she, perhaps, really more of an idea than I who it could be? She betrayed nothing of what her intuition told her, but I felt sure that, even though she knew nothing, there was at least something she feared.

At last we arrived at Dr. Mead's and I handed her out of the car and into the tastefully furnished little house. There was an air of quietness about it that often indefinably pervades a house in which there is illness or a tragedy.

"May I—see him?" pleaded Miss Winslow, as Dr. Mead placed a chair for her.

I wondered what he would have done if there had been some good reason why he should resist the pleading of her deep eyes.

"Why—er—for a minute—yes," he answered. "Later, soon, he may see visitors longer, but just now I think for a few hours the less he is disturbed the better."

The doctor excused himself for a moment to look at his patient and prepare him for the visit. Meanwhile Miss Winslow waited in the reception room downstairs, still very pale and nervous.

Warrington was in much less pain now than he had been when we left and Dr. Mead decided that, since the nurse had made him so much more comfortable, no further drug was necessary. In fact as his natural vitality due to his athletic habits and clean living asserted itself, it seemed as if his injuries which at first had looked so serious were not likely to prove as bad as the doctor had anticipated.

Still, he was badly enough as it was. The new nurse smoothed out his pillows and deftly tried to conceal as much as she could that would suggest how badly he was injured and at last Violet Winslow was allowed to enter the room where the poor boy lay.

Miss Winslow never for a moment let her wonderful self-control fail her. Quickly and noiselessly, like a ministering angel, she seemed to float rather than walk over the space from the door to the bed.

As she bent over him and whispered, "Mortimer!" the simple tone seemed to have an almost magic effect on him.

He opened his eyes which before had been languidly closed and gazed up at her face as if he saw a vision. Slowly the expression on his face changed as he realized that it was indeed Violet herself. In spite of the pain of his hurts which must have been intense a smile played over his features, as if he realized that it would never do to let her know how serious had been his condition.

As she bent over her hand had rested on the white covers of the bed. Feebly, in spite of the bandages that swathed the arm nearest her, he put out his own brawny hand and rested it on hers. She did not withdraw it, but passed the other hand gently over his throbbing forehead. Never have I seen a greater transformation in an invalid than was evident in Mortimer Warrington. No tonic in all the pharmacopoeia of Dr. Mead could have worked a more wonderful change.

Not a word was said by either Warrington or Violet for several seconds. They seemed content just to gaze into each other's faces, oblivious to us.

Warrington was the first to break the silence, in answer to

what he knew must be her unspoken question.

"Your aunt—gambling," he murmured feebly, trying hard to connect his words so to appear not so badly off as he had when he had spoken before. "I didn't know—till they told me—that the estate owned it—was coming to tell you—going to cancel the lease—close it up—no one ever lose money there again—"

The words, jerky though they were, cost him a great physical effort to say. She seemed to realize it, but there was a look of triumph on her face as she understood.

She had not been mistaken. Warrington was all that she had thought him to be.

He was looking eagerly into her face and as he looked he read in it the answer to the questionings that had sent him off in the early hours of the morning on his fateful ride to Tuxedo.

Dr. Mead cleared his throat. Miss Winslow recognised it as a signal that the time was growing short for the interview.

Reluctantly, she withdrew her hand from his, their eyes met another instant, and with a hasty word of sympathy and encouragement she left the room, conscious now that other eyes were watching.

"Oh, to think it was to tell me that that he got into it all," she cried, as she sank into a deep chair in the reception room, endeavouring not to give way to her feelings, now that the strain was off and she had no longer to keep a brave face. "I—I feel guilty!"

"I wouldn't say that," soothed Garrick. "Who knows? Perhaps

if he had stayed in the city—they might have succeeded,—whoever it was back of this thing."

She looked up at Garrick, startled, I thought, with the same expression I had seen when she turned her face away in the car and I got the impression that she felt more than she knew of the case.

"I may—see—Mr. Warrington again soon?" she asked, now again mistress of her feelings after Garrick's interruption that had served to take her mind off a morbid aspect of the affair.

"Surely," agreed Dr. Mead. "I expect his progress to be rapid after this."

"Thank you," she murmured, as she slowly rose and prepared to make the return trip to her aunt's home.

"Oh, Mr. Garrick," she confided, as he helped her on with the wraps she had thrown carelessly on a chair when she entered, "I can't help it—I do feel guilty. Perhaps he thinks I am—like Aunt Emma—"

"Perhaps it was quite as much to convince your aunt as you that he took the trip," suggested Garrick.

Miss Winslow understood. "Why is it," she murmured, "that sometimes people with the best intentions manage to bring about things that are—more terrible?"

Garrick smiled. Quite evidently she and her aunt were not exactly in tune. He said nothing.

As for Dr. Mead he seemed really pleased, for the patient had brightened up considerably after even the momentary glimpse he had had of Violet. Altogether I felt that although they had seen each other only for a moment, it had done both good. Miss Winslow's fears had been quieted and Warrington had been encouraged by the realisation that, in spite of its disastrous ending, his journey had accomplished its purpose anyway.

There was, as Dr. Mead assured us, every prospect now that Warrington would pull through after the murderous assault that had been made on him.

We saw Miss Winslow safely off on her return trip, much relieved by the promise of the doctor that she might call once a day to see how the patient was getting along.

Warrington was now resting more easily than he had since the accident and Garrick, having exhausted the possibilities of investigation at the scene of the accident, announced that he would return to the city.

At the railroad terminus he called up both the apartment and the office in order to find out whether we had had any visitors during our absence. No one had called at the apartment, but the office boy downtown said that there was a man who had called and was coming back again.

A half hour or so later when we arrived at the office we found McBirney seated there, patiently determined to find Garrick.

Evidently the news of the assault on Warrington had travelled fast, for the first thing McBirney wanted to know was how it happened and how his client was. In a few words Garrick told him as much about it as was necessary. McBirney listened attentively, but we could see that he was bursting with his own budget of news.

"And, McBirney," concluded Garrick, without going into the question of the marks of the tires, "most remarkable of all, I am convinced that the car in which his assailant rode was no other than the Mercedes that was stolen from Warrington in the first place."

"Say," exclaimed McBirney in surprise, "that car must be all over at once!"

"Why—what do you mean?"

"You know I have my own underground sources of information," explained the detective with pardonable pride at adding even a rumour to the budget of news. "Of course you can't be certain of such things, but one of my men, who is scouting around the Tenderloin looking for what he can find, tells me that he saw a car near that gambling joint on Forty-eighth Street and that it may have been the repainted and renumbered Warrington car—at least it tallies with the description that we got from the garage keeper in north Jersey.

"Did he see who drove it?" asked Garrick eagerly.

"Not very well. It was a short, undersized man, as nearly as he could make out. Someone whom he did not recognize jumped in it from the gambling house and they disappeared. Even though my man, his suspicions aroused, tried to follow them in a taxicab they managed to leave him behind."

"In what direction did they go?" asked Garrick.

"Toward the West Side—where those fly-by-night garages are all located."

"Or, perhaps, the Jersey ferries," suggested Garrick.

"Well, I thought you might like to know about this under-sized driver," said McBirney a little sulkily because Garrick had not displayed as much enthusiasm as he expected.

"I do," hastened Garrick. "Of course I do. And it may prove to be a very important clew. But I was just running ahead of your story. The undersized man couldn't have figured in the case afterward, assuming that it was the car. He must have left it, probably in the city. Have you any idea who it could be?"

"Not unless he might be an employee or a keeper of one of those night-hawk garages," persisted McBirney. "That is possible."

"Quite," agreed Garrick.

McBirney had delivered his own news and in turn had received ours, or at least such of it as Garrick chose to tell at present. He was apparently satisfied and rose to go.

"Keep after that undersized fellow, will you?" asked Garrick. "If you could find out who he is and he should happen to be connected with one of those garages we might get on the right trail at last."

"I will," promised McBirney. "He's evidently an expert driver of motor cars himself; my man could see that."

McBirney had gone. Garrick sat for several minutes gazing squarely at me. Then he leaned back in his chair, with his hands behind his head.

"Mark my words, Marshall," he observed slowly, "someone connected with that gambling joint in some way has got wind of the fact that Warrington is going to revoke the lease and close it up. We've got to beat them to it—that's all."

CHAPTER IX

THE RAID

Garrick was evidently turning over and over in his mind some plan of action.

"This thing has gone just about far enough," he remarked meditatively, looking at his watch. It was now well along in the afternoon.

"But what do you intend doing?" I asked, regarding the whole affair so far as a hopeless mystery from which I could not see that we had extracted so much as a promising clew.

"Doing?" he echoed. "Why, there is only one thing to do, and that is to take the bull by the horns, to play the game without any further attempt at finessing. I shall see Dillon, get a warrant, and raid that gambling place—that's all."

I had no counter suggestion to offer. In fact the plan rather appealed to me. If any blow were to be struck it must be just a little bit ahead of any that the gamblers anticipated, and this was a blow they would not expect if they already had wind of Warrington's intention to cancel the lease.

Garrick called up Dillon and made an appointment to meet

him early in the evening, without telling him what was afoot.

"Meet me down at police headquarters, Tom," was all that Garrick said to me. "I want to work here at the office for a little while, first, testing a new contrivance, or, rather, an old one that I think may be put to a new use."

Meanwhile I decided to employ my time by visiting some newspaper friends that I had known a long time on the Star, one of the most enterprising papers in the city. Fortunately I found my friend, Davenport, the managing editor, at his desk and ready to talk in the infrequent lulls that came in his work.

"What's on your mind, Marshall?" he asked as I sat down and began to wonder how he ever conducted his work in the choatic clutter of stuff on the top of his desk.

"I can't tell you—yet, Davenport," I explained carefully, "but it's a big story and when it breaks I'll promise that the Star has the first chance at it. I'm on the inside—working with that young detective, Garrick, you know."

"Garrick—Garrick," he repeated. "Oh, yes, that fellow who came back from abroad with a lot of queer ideas. I remember. We had an interview with him when he left the steamer. Good stuff, too,—but what do you think of him? Is he—on the level?"

"On the level and making good," I answered confidently. "I'm not at liberty to tell much about it now, but—well, the reason I came in was to find out what you could tell me about a Miss Winslow,—Violet Winslow and her aunt, Mrs. Beekman de Lancey."

"The Miss Winslow who is reported engaged to young

Warrington?" he repeated. "The gossip is that he has cut out Angus Forbes, entirely."

I had hesitated to mention all the names at once, but I need not have done so, for on such things, particularly the fortunes in finance and love of such a person as Warrington, the eyes of the press were all-seeing.

"Yes," I answered carefully, "that's the Miss Winslow. What do you know of her?"

"Well," he replied, fumbling among the papers on his desk, "all I know is that in the social set to which she belongs our society reporters say that of all the young fellows who have set out to capture her—and she's a deuced pretty girl, even in the pictures we have published—it seems to have come down to Mortimer Warrington and Angus Forbes. Of course, as far as we newspapermen are concerned, the big story for us would be in the engagement of young Warrington. The eyes of people are fixed on him just now—the richest young man in the country, and all that sort of thing, you know. Seems to be a pretty decent sort of fellow, too, I believe—democratic and keen on other things besides tango and tennis. Oh, there's the thing I was hunting for. Mrs. de Lancey's a nut on gambling, I believe. Read that. It's a letter that came to us from her this morning."

It was written in the stilted handwriting of a generation ago and read:

"To the Editor of the Star, Dear Sir:—I believe that your paper prides itself on standing for reform and against the grafters. If that is so, why do you not join in the crusade to suppress gambling in New York? For the love that you must still bear towards your own mother, listen to the stories of other mothers torn by anxiety for their sons and daughters, and if there is any justice or righteousness in this great city close up those gambling hells that are sending to ruin scores of our finest young men—and women. You have taken up other fights against gambling and vice. Take up this one that appeals to women of wealth and social position. I know them and they are as human as mothers in any other station in life. Oh, if there is any way, close up these gilded society resorts that are dissipating the fortunes of many parents, ruining young men and women, and, in one case I know of, slowly bringing to the grave a grey-haired widow as worthy of protection as any mother of the poor whose plea has closed up a little poolroom or policy shop. One place I have in mind is at—West Forty-eighth Street. Investigate it, but keep this confidential.

"Sincerely,

"(MRS.) EMMA DE LANCEY."

"Do you know anything about it?" I asked casually handing the letter back.

"Only by hearsay. I understand it is the crookedest gambling joint in the city, at least judging by the stories they tell of the losses there. And so beastly aristocratic, too. They tell me young Forbes has lost a small fortune there—but I don't know how true it is. We get hundreds of these daintily perfumed and monogramed little missives in the course of a year."

"You mean Angus Forbes?" I asked.

"Yes," replied the managing editor, "the fellow that they say has been trying to capture your friend Miss Winslow."

I did not reply for the moment. Forbes, I had already learned, was deeply in debt. Was it part of his plan to get control of the little fortune of Violet to recoup his losses?

"Do you know Mrs. de Lancey?" pursued the editor.

"No—not yet," I answered. "I was just wondering what sort of person she is."

"Oh I suppose she's all right," he answered, "but they say she's pretty straight-laced—that cards and all sorts of dissipation are an obsession with her."

"Well," I argued, "there might be worse things than that."

"That's right," he agreed. "But I don't believe that such a puritanical atmosphere is—er—just the place to bring up a young woman like Violet Winslow."

I said nothing. It did not seem to me that Mrs. de Lancey had succeeded in killing the natural human impulses in Violet, though perhaps the girl was not as well versed in some of the ways of the world as others of her set. Still, I felt that her own natural common sense would protect her, even though she had been kept from a knowledge of much that in others of her set was part of their "education."

My friend's telephone had been tinkling constantly during the conversation and I saw that as the time advanced he was getting more and more busy. I thanked Davenport and excused myself.

At least I had learned something about those who were concerned in the case. As I rode uptown I could not help thinking of Violet Winslow and her apparently intuitive fear concerning Warrington. I wondered how much she really knew about Angus Forbes. Undoubtedly he had not hesitated to express his own feelings toward her. Had she penetrated beneath the honeyed words he must have spoken to her? Was it that she feared that all things are fair in war and love and that the favour she must have bestowed on Warrington might have roused the jealousy of some of his rivals for her affections?

I found no answer to my speculations, but a glance at my watch told me that it was nearing the time of my appointment with Guy.

A few minutes later I jumped off the car at Headquarters and met Garrick, waiting for me in the lower hall. As we ascended the broad staircase to the second floor, where Dillon's office was, I told him briefly of what I had discovered.

"The old lady will have her wish," he replied grimly as I related the incident of the letter to the editor. "I wonder just how much she really does know of that place. I hope it isn't enough to set her against Warrington. You know people like that are often likely to conceive violent prejudices—and then refuse to believe something that's all but proved about someone else."

There was no time to pursue the subject further for we had reached Dillon's office and were admitted immediately.

"What's the news?" asked Dillon greeting us cordially.

"Plenty of it," returned Garrick, hastily sketching over what had transpired since we had seen him last.

Garrick had scarcely begun to outline what he intended to do when I could see from the commissioner's face that he was very sceptical of success.

"Herman tells me," he objected, "that the place is mighty well barricaded. We haven't tried raiding it yet, because you know the new plan is not only to raid those places, but first to watch them, trace out some of the regular habitues, and then to be able to rope them in in case we need them as evidence. Herman has been getting that all in shape so that when the case comes to trial, there'll be no slip-up."

"If that's all you want, I can put my finger on some of the wildest scions of wealth that you will ever need for witnesses," Garrick replied confidently.

"Well," pursued Dillon diffidently, "how are you going to pull it off, down through the sky-light, or up through the cellar?"

"Oh, Dillon," returned Garrick reproachfully, "that's unworthy of you."

"But, Garrick," persisted Dillon, "don't you know that it is a veritable National City Bank for protection. It isn't one of those common gambling joints. It's proof against all the old methods. Axes and sledgehammers would make no impression there. Why, that place has been proved bomb-proof—bomb-proof, sir. You remember recently the so-call 'gamblers' war' in which some rivals exploded a bomb on the steps because the proprietor of this place resented their intrusion uptown from the lower East Side, with their gunmen and lobbygows? It did more damage to the house next door than to the gambling joint."

Dillon paused a moment to enumerate the difficulties. "You can get past the outside door all right. But inside is the famous ice-box door. It's no use to try it at all unless you can pass that door with reasonable quickness. All the evidence you will get will be of an innocent social club room downstairs. And you can't get on the other side of that door by strategy, either. It is strategy-proof. The system of lookouts is perfect. Herman—"

"Can't help it," interrupted Garrick, "we've got to go over Herman's head this time. I'll guarantee you all the evidence you'll ever need."

Dillon and Garrick faced each other for a moment.

It was a supreme test of Dillon's sincerity.

Finally he spoke slowly. "All right," he said, as if at last the die were cast and Garrick had carried his point, "but how are you going to do it? Won't you need some men with axes and crowbars?"

"No, indeed, almost shouted Garrick as Dillon made a motion as if to find out who were available. "I've been preparing a little surprise in my office this afternoon for just such a case. It's a rather cumbersome arrangement and I've brought it along stowed away in a taxicab outside. I don't want anyone else to know about the raid until the last moment. Just before we begin the rough stuff, you can call up and have the reserves started around. That is all I shall want."

"Very well," agreed Dillon, after a moment.

He did not seem to relish the scheme, but he had promised at the outset to play fair and he had no disposition to go back on his word now in favor even of his judgment.

"First of all," he planned, "we'll have to drop in on a judge and get a warrant to protect us."

Garrick hastily gave me instructions what to do and I started uptown immediately, while they went to secure the secret warrant.

I had been stationed on the corner which was not far from the Forty-eighth Street gambling joint that we were to raid. I had a keen sense of wickedness as I stood there with other loiterers watching the passing throng under the yellow flare of the flaming arc light.

It was not difficult now to loiter about unnoticed because the streets were full of people, all bent on their own pleasure and not likely to notice one person more or less who stopped to watch the passing throng.

From time to time I cast a quick glance at the house down the street, in order to note who was going in.

It must have been over an hour that I waited. It was after ten, and it became more difficult to watch who was going into the gambling joint. In fact, several times the street was so blocked that I could not see very well. But I did happen to catch a glimpse of one familiar figure across the street from me.

It was Angus Forbes. Where he kept himself in the daytime I did not know, but he seemed to emerge at night, like a rat, seeking what to him was now food and drink. I watched him narrowly as he turned the corner, but there was no use in being too inquisitive. He was bound as certainly for the gambling joint as a moth would have headed toward one of the arc lights. Evidently Forbes was making a vocation of gambling.

Just then a taxicab pulled up hurriedly at the curb near where I was standing and a hand beckoned me, on the side away from the gambling house.

Arthur B. Reeve

I sauntered over and looked in through the open window. It was Garrick with Dillon sunk back into the dark corner of the cab, so as not to be seen.

"Jump in!" whispered Garrick, opening the door. "We have the warrant all right. Has anything happened? No suspicion yet?"

I did so and reassured Garrick while the cab started on a blind cruise around the block.

On the floor was a curiously heavy instrument, on which I had stubbed my toe as I entered. I surmised that it must have been the thing which Garrick had brought from his office, but in the darkness I could not see what it was, nor was there a chance to ask a question.

"Stop here," ordered Garrick, as we passed a drug store with a telephone booth.

Dillon jumped out and disappeared into the booth.

"He is calling the reserves from the nearest station," fretted Garrick. "Of course, we have to do that to cover the place, but we'll have to work quickly now, for I don't know how fast a tip may travel in this subterranean region. Here, I'll pay the taxi charges now and save some time."

A moment later Dillon rejoined us, his face perspiring from the closeness of the air in the booth.

"Now to that place on Forty-eighth Street, and we're square," ordered Garrick to the driver, mentioning the address. "Quick!"

There had been, we could see, no chance for a tip to be given that a raid was about to be pulled off. We could see that, as Garrick and I jumped out of the cab and mounted the steps.

The door was closed to us, however. Only someone like Warrington who was known there could have got us in peacefully, until we had become known in the place. Yet though there had been no tip, the lookout on the other side of the door, with his keen nose, had seemed to scent trouble.

He had retreated and, we knew, had shut the inside, heavy door—perhaps even had had time already to give the alarm inside.

The sharp rap of a small axe which Garrick had brought sounded on the flimsy outside door, in quick staccato. There was a noise and scurry of feet inside and we could hear the locks and bolts being drawn.

Banging, ripping, tearing, the thin outer door was easily forced. Disregarding the melee I leaped through the wreckage with Garrick. The "ice-box" door barred all further progress. How was Garrick to surmount this last and most formidable barrier?

"A raid! A raid!" cried a passer-by.

Another instant, and the cry, taken up by others, brought a crowd swarming around from Broadway, as if it were noon instead of midnight.

CHAPTER X

THE GAMBLING DEBT

There was no time to be lost now. Down the steps again dashed Garrick, after our expected failure both to get in peaceably and to pass the ice-box door by force. This time Dillon emerged from the cab with him. Together they were carrying the heavy apparatus up the steps.

They set it down close to the door and I scrutinized it carefully. It looked, at first sight, like a short stubby piece of iron, about eighteen inches high. It must have weighed fifty or sixty pounds. Along one side was a handle, and on the opposite side an adjustable hook with a sharp, wide prong.

Garrick bent down and managed to wedge the hook into the little space between the sill and the bottom of the ice-box door. Then he began pumping on the handle, up and down, up and down, as hard as he could.

Meanwhile the crowd that had begun to collect was getting larger. Dillon went through the form of calling on them for aid, but the call was met with laughter. A Tenderloin crowd has no use for raids, except as a spectacle. Between us we held them back, while Garrick worked. The crowd jeered.

It was the work of only a few seconds, however, before Garrick changed the jeers to a hearty round of exclamations of surprise. The door seemed to be lifted up, literally, until some of its bolts and hinges actually bulged and cracked. It was being crushed, like the flimsy outside door, before the unwonted attack.

Upwards, by fractions of an inch, by millimeters, the door was being forced. There was such straining and stress of materials that I really began to wonder whether the building itself would stand it.

"Scientific jimmying," gasped Garrick, as the door bulged more and more and seemed almost to threaten to topple in at any moment.

I looked at the stubby little cylinder with its short stump of a lever. Garrick had taken it out now and had wedged it horizontally between the ice-box door and the outer stonework of the building itself. Then he jammed some pieces of wood in to wedge it tighter and again began to pump at the handle vigorously.

"What is it?" I asked, almost in awe at the titanic power of the apparently insignificant little thing.

"My scientific sledgehammer," he panted, still working the lever more vigorously than ever backward and forward. "In other words, a hydraulic ram. There is no swinging of axes or wielding of crow-bars necessary any more, Dillon, in breaking down a door like this. Such things are obsolete. This little jimmy, if you want to call it that, has a power of ten tons. I think that's about enough."

It seemed as if the door were buckling and being literally wrenched off its hinges by the irresistible ten-ton punch of the hydraulic ram.

Garrick sprang back, grasping me by the arm and pulling me too. But there was no need of caution. What was left of the door swung back on its loosened hinges, seemed to tremble a moment, and then, with a dull thud crashed down on the beautiful green marble of the reception hall, reverberating.

We peered beyond. Inside all was darkness. At the very first sign of trouble the lights had been switched out downstairs. It was deserted. There was no answer to our shouts. It was as silent as a tomb.

The clang of bells woke the rapid echoes. The crowd parted. It was the patrol wagons, come just in time, full of reserves, at Dillon's order. They swarmed up the steps, for there was nothing to do now, in the limelight of the public eye, except their duty. Besides Dillon was there, too.

"Here," he ordered huskily, "four of you fellows jump into each of the next door houses and run up to the roof. Four more men go through to the rear of this house. The rest stay here and await orders," he directed, detailing them off quickly, as he endeavoured to grasp the strange situation.

On both sides of the street heads were out of windows. On other houses the steps were full of spectators. Thousands of people must have swarmed in the street. It was pandemonium.

Yet inside the house into which we had just broken it was all darkness and silence.

The door had yielded to the scientific sledge-hammering where it would have shattered, otherwise, all the axes in the department. What was next?

Garrick jumped briskly over the wreckage into the building. Instead of the lights and gayety which we had seen on the previous night, all was black mystery. The robbers' cave yawned before us. I think we were all prepared for some sort of gunplay, for we knew the crooks to be desperate characters. As we followed Garrick closely we were surprised to encounter not even physical force.

Someone struck a light. Garrick, groping about in the shadows, found the switch, and one after another the lights in the various rooms winked up.

I have seldom seen such confusion as greeted us as, with Dillon waiving his "John Doe" warrant over his head, we hurried upstairs to the main hall on the second floor, where the greater part of the gambling was done. Furniture was overturned and broken, and there had been no time to remove the heavier gambling apparatus. Playing cards, however, chips, racing sheets from the afternoon, dice, everything portable and tangible and small enough to be carried had disappeared.

But the greatest surprise of all was in store. Though we had seen no one leave by any of the doors, nor by the doors of any of the houses on the block, nor by the roofs, or even by the back yard, according to the report of the police who had been sent in that direction, there was not a living soul in the house from roof to cellar. Search as we did, we could find not one of the scores of people whom I had seen enter in the course of the evening while I was watching on the corner.

Dillon, ever mindful of some of the absurd rules of evidence in such cases laid down by the courts, had had an official photographer summoned and he was proceeding from room to room, snapping pictures of apparatus that was left in place and preserving a film record of the condition of things generally.

Arthur B. Reeve

Garrick was standing ruefully beside the roulette wheel at which so many fortunes had been dissipated.

"Get me an axe," he asked of one of Dillon's men who was passing.

With a well-directed blow he smashed the wheel.

"Look," he exclaimed, "this is what they were up against."

His forefinger indicated an ingenious but now twisted and tangled series of minute wires and electro-magnets in the delicate mechanism now broken open before us. Delicate brushes led the current into the wheel.

With another blow of the axe, Garrick disclosed wires running down through the leg of the table to the floor and under the carpet to buttons operated by the man who ran the game.

"What does it mean?" I asked blankly.

"It means," he returned, "that they had little enough chance to win at a straight game of roulette. But this wheel wasn't even straight with all the odds in favor of the bank, as they are naturally. This game was electrically controlled. Others are mechanically controlled by what are called the 'mule's ear,' and other devices. You CAN'T win. These wires and magnets can be made to attract the little ball into any pocket the operator desires. Each one of the pockets contains an electro-magnet. One set of electro-magnets in the red pockets is connected with one button under the carpet and a set of batteries. The other series of little magnets in the black pockets is connected with another button and the batteries."

He had picked up the little ball. "This ball," he said as he examined it, "is not really of ivory, but of a composition that looks like ivory, coating a hollow, soft-iron ball inside. Soft iron is attracted by an electro-magnet. Whichever set of magnets is energized attracts the ball and by this simple method it is in the power of the operator to let the ball go to red or black as he may wish. Other similar arrangements control the odd or even, and other combinations, also from push buttons. There isn't an honest gambling machine in the whole place. The whole thing is crooked from start to finish,—the men, the machines,—"

"Then a fellow never had a chance?" repeated Dillon.

"Not a chance," emphasized Garrick.

We gathered about and gazed at magnets and wires, the buttons and switches. He did not need to say anything more to expose the character of the place.

Amazing as we found everything about us in the palace of crooks, nothing made so deep an impression on me as the fact that it was deserted. It seemed as if the gamblers had disappeared as though in a fairy tale. Search room after room as Dillon's men did they were unable to find a living thing.

One of the men had discovered, back of the gambling rooms on the second floor, a little office evidently used by those who ran the joint. It was scantily furnished, as though its purpose might have been merely a place where they could divide up the profits in private. A desk, a cabinet and a safe, besides a couple of chairs, were all that the room contained.

Someone, however, had done some quick work in the little office during those minutes while Garrick was opening the great ice-box door with his hydraulic ram, for on every side were scattered papers, the desk had been rifled, and even

Arthur B. Reeve

from the safe practically everything of any value had been removed. It was all part of the general scheme of things in the gambling joint. Practically nothing that was evidential that could be readily removed had been left. Whoever had planned the place must have been a genius as far as laying out precautions against a raid were concerned.

Garrick, Dillon and I ran hastily through some scattered correspondence and other documents that spilled out from some letter files on the floor, but as far as I could make out there was nothing of any great importance that had been overlooked.

Dillon ordered the whole mass to be bundled up and taken off when the other paraphernalia was removed so that it could be gone through at our leisure, and the search continued.

From the "office" a staircase led down by a back way and we followed it, looking carefully to see where it led.

A low exclamation from Garrick arrested our attention. In a curve between landings he had kicked something and had bent down to pick it up. An electric pocket flashlight which one of the men had picked up disclosed under its rays a package of papers evidently dropped by someone who was carrying away in haste an armful of stuff.

"Markers with the house," exclaimed Garrick as he ran over the contents of the package hurriedly. "I. O. U.'s for various amounts and all initialed—for several hundred thousands. Hello, here's a bunch with an 'F.' That must mean Forbes—thousands of dollars worth."

The markers were fastened together with a slip in order to separate them from the others, evidently.

Garrick was hastily totalling them up and they seemed to amount to a tidy sum.

"How can he ever pay?" I asked, amazed as the sum crept on upward in the direction of six figures.

"Don't you see that they're cancelled?" interjected Garrick, still adding.

I had not examined them closely, but as I now bent over to do so I saw that each bore the words, "Paid by W."

Warrington himself had settled the gambling debts of his friend!

In still greater amazement I continued to look and found that they all bore dates from several weeks before, down to within a few days. The tale they told was eloquent. Forbes, his own fortune gone, had gambled until rescued by his friend. Even that had not been sufficient to curb his mania. He had kept right on, hoping insanely to recoup. And the gamblers had been willing to take a chance with him, knowing that they already had so much of his money that they could not possibly lose.

A horrid thought flashed over me. What if he had really planned to pay his losses by marrying a girl with a fortune? Forbes was the sort who would have gambled on even that slender prospect.

As we stood on the landing while Garrick went over the markers, I found myself wondering, even, where Forbes had been that night after he hurried away from us at the ladies' poolroom and Warrington had taken the journey that had ended so disastrously for him. The more I learned of what had been taking place, the more I saw that Warrington stood out as a gentleman. Undoubtedly Violet Winslow had heard, had been informed by some kind unknown of the slight lapses of Warrington. I felt sure that the gross delinquencies of Forbes were concealed from her and from her aunt, at least as far as Warrington had it in his power to shield the man who was his friend—and rival.

The voice of Dillon recalled me from a train of pure speculation to the more practical work in hand before us.

"Well, at any rate, we've got evidence enough to protect ourselves and close the place, even if we didn't make any captures," congratulated Dillon, as he rejoined us, after a momentary excursion from which he returned still blinking from the effects of the flashlight powders which his photo-grapher had been using freely. "After we get all the pictures of the place, I'll have the stuff here removed to head-quarters—and it won't be handed back on any order of the courts, either, if I can help it!"

Garrick had shoved the markers into his pocket and now was leading the way downstairs.

"Still, Dillon," he remarked, as we followed, "that doesn't shed any light on the one remaining problem. How did they all manage to get out so quickly?"

We had reached the basement which contained the kitchens for the buffet and quarters for the servants. A hasty excursion into the littered back yard under the guidance of Dillon's men who had been sent around that way netted us nothing in the way of information. They had not made their escape over the back fences. Such a number of people would certainly have left some trail, and there was none.

We looked at Garrick, perplexed, and he remarked, with

sudden energy, "Let's take a look at the cellar."

As we groped down the final stairway into the cellar, it was only too evident that at last he had guessed right. Down in the subterranean depths we quickly discovered, at the rear, a sheet-iron door. Battering it down was the work of but a moment for the little ram. Beyond it, where we expected to see a yawning tunnel, we found nothing but a pile of bricks and earth and timbers that had been used for shoring.

There had been a tunnel, but the last man who had gone through had evidently exploded a small dynamite cartridge, and the walls had been caved in. It was impossible to follow it until its course could be carefully excavated with proper tools in the daylight.

We had captured the stronghold of gambling in New York, but the gamblers had managed to slip out of our grasp, at least for the present.

CHAPTER XI

THE GANGSTER'S GARAGE

"I have it," exclaimed Garrick, as we were retracing our steps upstairs from the dank darkness of the cellar. "I would be willing to wager that that tunnel runs back from this house to that pool-room for women which we visited on Forty-seventh Street, Marshall. That must be the secret exit. Don't you see, it could be used in either direction."

We climbed the stairs and stood again in the wreck of things, taking a hasty inventory of what was left, in hope of uncovering some new clew, even by chance.

Garrick shook his head mournfully.

"They had just time enough," he remarked, "to destroy about everything they wanted to and carry off the rest."

"All except the markers," I corrected.

"That was just a lucky chance," he returned. "Still, it throws an interesting sidelight on the case."

"It doesn't add much in my estimation to the character of Forbes," I ventured, voicing my own suspicions.

The telephone bell rang before Garrick had a chance to reply. Evidently in their haste they had not had time to cut the wires or to spread the news, yet, of the raid. Someone who knew nothing of what had happened was calling up.

Garrick quickly unhooked the receiver, with a hasty motion to us to remain silent.

"Hello," we heard him answer. "Yes, this is it. Who is this?"

He had disguised his voice. We waited anxiously and watched his face to gather what response he received.

"The deuce!" he exclaimed, with his hand over the transmitter so that his voice would not be heard at the other end.

"What's the matter?" I asked eagerly.

"Whoever he was," replied Garrick, "he was too keen for me. He caught on. There must have been some password or form that they used which we don't know, for he hung up the receiver almost as soon as he heard me."

Garrick waited a minute or two. Then he whistled into, the transmitter. It was done apparently to see whether there was anyone listening. But there was no answer. The man was gone.

"Operator, operator!" Guy was calling, insistently moving the hook up and down rapidly. "Yes—I want Central. Central, can you tell me what number that was which just called up?"

We all waited anxiously to learn whether the girl could find out or not.

"Bleecker seven—one—eight—o? Thank you very much. Give me information, please."

Again we waited as Garrick tried to trace the call out.

"Hello! What is the street address of Bleecker seven—one—eight—o? Three hundred West Sixth. Thank you. A garage? Good-bye."

"A garage?" echoed Dillon, his ears almost going up as he realized the importance of the news.

"Yes," cried Garrick, himself excited. "Tom, call a cab. Let us hustle down there as quickly as we can."

"One of those garages on the lower West Side," I heard Dillon say as I left. "Perhaps they did work for the gambling joint—sent drunks home, got rid of tough customers and all that. You know already that there are some pretty tough places down there. This is bully. I shouldn't be surprised if it gave us a line on the stealing of Warrington's car at last."

I found a cab and Dillon and Garrick joined me in it.

"I tried to get McBirney," said Garrick as we prepared to start on our new quest, "but he was out, and the night operator at his place didn't seem to know where he was. But if they can locate him, I imagine he'll be around at least shortly after we get there. I left the address."

Dillon had issued his final orders to his raiders about guarding the raided gambling joint and stationing a man at the door. A moment later we were off, threading our way through the crowd which in spite of the late hour still lingered to gape at the place.

On the way down we speculated much on the possibility that we might be going on a wild goose chase. But the very circumstances of the call and the promptness with which the man who had called had seemed to sense when something was wrong and to ring off seemed to point to the fact that we had uncovered a good lead of some kind.

After a quick run downtown through the deserted avenues, we entered a series of narrow and sinuous streets that wound through some pretty tough looking neighborhoods. On the street corners were saloons that deserved no better name than common groggeries. They were all vicious looking joints and uniformly seemed to violate the law about closing. The fact was that they impressed one as though it would be as much as one's life was worth even to enter them with respectable looking clothes on.

The further we proceeded into the tortuous twists of streets that stamp the old Greenwich village with a character all its own, the worse it seemed to get. Decrepit relics of every style of architecture from almost the earliest times in the city stood out in the darkness, like so many ghosts.

"Anyone who would run a garage down here," remarked Garrick, "deserves to be arrested on sight."

"Except possibly for commercial vehicles," I ventured, looking at the warehouses here and there.

"There are no commercial vehicles out at this hour," added Garrick dryly.

At last our cab turned down a street that was particularly dark.

"This is it," announced Garrick, tapping on the glass for the driver to stop at the corner. "We had better get out and walk the rest of the way."

The garage which we sought proved to be nothing but an old brick stable. It was of such a character that even charity could not have said that it had seen much better days for generations. It was dark, evil looking. Except for a slinking figure here and there in the distance the street about us was deserted. Even our footfalls echoed and Garrick warned us to tread softly. I longed for the big stick, that went with the other half of the phrase.

He paused a moment to observe the place. It was near the corner and a dim-lighted Raines law saloon on the next cross street ran back almost squarely to the stable walls, leaving a narrow yard. Apparently the garage itself had been closed for the night, if, indeed, it was ever regularly open. Anyone who wanted to use it must have carried a key, I surmised.

We crossed over stealthily. Garrick put his ear to an ordinary sized door which had been cut out of the big double swinging doors of the stable, and listened.

Not a sound.

Dillon, with the instinct of the roundsman in him still, tried the handle of the door gently. To our surprise it moved. I could not believe that anyone could have gone away and left it open, trusting that the place would not be looted by the neighbours before he returned. I felt instinctively that there must be somebody there, in spite of the darkness.

The commissioner pushed in, however, followed closely by both of us, prepared for an on-rush or a hand-to-hand struggle with anything, man or beast.

A quick succession of shots greeted us. I do not recall feeling the slightest sensation of pain, but with a sickening dizziness in the head I can just vaguely remember that I sank down on the oil and grease of the floor. I did not fall. It seemed as if I had time to catch myself and save, perhaps, a fractured skull. But then it was all blank.

It seemed an age, though it could not have been more than ten minutes later when I came to. I felt an awful, choking sensation in my throat which was dry and parched. My lungs seemed to rasp my very ribs, as I struggled for breath. Garrick was bending anxiously over me, himself pale and gasping yet. The air was reeking with a smell that I did not understand.

"Thank heaven, you're all right," he exclaimed, with much relief, as he helped me struggle up on my feet. My head was still in a whirl as he assisted me over to a cushioned seat in one of the automobiles standing there. "Now I'll go back to Dillon," he added, out of breath from the superhuman efforts he was putting forth both for us and to keep himself together. "Wh—what's the matter? What happened?" I gasped, gripping the back of the cushion to steady myself. "Am I wounded? Where was I hit? I—I don't feel anything—but, oh, my head and throat!"

I glanced over at Dillon. He was pale and white as a ghost, but I could see that he was breathing, though with difficulty. In the glare of the headlight of a car which Garrick had turned on him, he looked ghastly. I looked again to discover traces of blood. But there was none anywhere.

"We were all put out of business," muttered Garrick, as he worked over Dillon. Dillon opened his eyes blankly at last, then struggled up to his feet. "You got it worst, commissioner," remarked Garrick to him. "You were closest."

Arthur B. Reeve

"Got what?" he sputtered, "Was closest to what?"

We were all still choking over the peculiar odor in the fetid air about us.

"The bulletless gun," replied Garrick.

Dillon looked at him a moment incredulously, in spite even of his trying physical condition.

"It is a German invention," Garrick went on to explain, clearing his throat, "and shoots, instead of bullets, a stupefying gas which temporarily blinds and chokes its victims. The fellow who was in here didn't shoot bullets at us. He evidently didn't care about adding any more crimes to his list just now. Perhaps he thought that if he killed any of us there would be too much of a row. I'm glad it was as it was, anyway. He got us all, this way, before we knew it. Perhaps that was the reason he used the gun, for if he had shot one of us with a pistol I had my own automatic ready myself to blaze away. This way he got me, too.

"A stupefying gun!" repeated Dillon. "I should say so. I don't know what happened—yet," he added, blinking.

"I came to first," went on Garrick, now busily looking about, as we were all recovered. "I found that none of us was wounded, and so I guessed what had happened. However, while we were unconscious the villain, whoever he was, succeeded in running his car out of the garage and getting away. He locked the door after him, but I have managed to work it open again."

Garrick was now examining the floor of the garage, turning the headlight of the machine as much as he could on successive parts of the floor.

"By George, Tom," he exclaimed to me suddenly, "see those marks in the grease? Do you recognize them by this time? It is the same tire-mark again—Warrington's car—without a doubt!"

Dillon had taken the photographs which Garrick had made several days before from the prints left by the side of the road in New Jersey, and was comparing them himself with the marks on the floor of the garage, while Garrick explained them to him hurriedly, as he had already done to me.

"We are getting closer to him, every time,'" remarked Garrick. "Even if he did get away, we are on the trail and know that it is the right one. He could not have been at the gambling joint, or he would never have called up. Yet he must have known all about it. This has turned out better than I expected. I suppose you don't feel so, but you must think so."

It was difficult not to catch the contagion of Garrick's enthusiasm. Dillon grunted assent.

"This garage," he put in, looking it over critically, "must act as a fence for stolen cars and parts of cars. See, there over in the corner is the stuff for painting new license numbers. Here's enough material to rebuild a half dozen cars. Yes, this is one of the places that ought to interest you and McBirney, Garrick. I'll bet the fellow who owns this place is one of those who'd engage to sell you a second-hand car of any make you wanted to name. Then he'd go out on the street and hunt around until he got one. Of course, we'll find out his name, but I'll wager that when we get the nominal owner we won't be able to extract a thing from him in the way of actual facts."

Garrick had continued his examination of the floor. In a corner, near the back, he had picked up an empty shell of a cartridge. He held it down in the light of the car, and examined it long and carefully. As he turned it over and over he seemed to be carefully considering it. Finally, he dropped it carefully into his inside vest pocket, as though it were a rare treasure.

"As I said at the start," quoted Garrick, turning to me, "we might get a conviction merely on these cartridges. Anyhow, our man has escaped from here. You can be sure that he won't come back—perhaps never—certainly not at least for a long time, until he figures that this thing has completely blown over."

"I'm going to keep my eye on the place, just the same," stoutly insisted Dillon.

"Of course, by all means," reiterated Garrick. "The fact is, I expect our next important clew will come from this place. The only thing I want you to be careful of, Dillon, is not to be hasty and make an arrest."

"Not make an arrest?" queried Dillon, who still felt the fumes in his throat, and evidently longed to make someone pay the price—at least by giving him the satisfaction of conducting a "third degree" down at headquarters.

"No. You won't get the right man, and you may lose one who points straight at him. Take my advice. Watch the place. There's more to be gained by going at it cautiously. These people understand the old hammer-and-tongs game."

Just then the smaller outside door grated on its rusty hinges. We sprang to our feet, startled. Dillon leaped forward. Stupefying guns had no taming effect on his nationality.

"Well, commish, is that the way you greet an old friend?" laughed McBirney, as a threatened strangle-hold was narrowly averted and turned into a handshake. "How are you fellows? I got your message, Garrick, and thought I'd drop around. What's the matter? You all look as if you'd been drawn through a wringer."

Briefly, to the accompaniment of many expressions of astonishment from the insurance detective, Garrick related what had happened, from the raid to the gas-gun.

"Well," gasped McBirney, sniffing the remains of the gas in the air, "this is some place, isn't it? Neat, cozy, well-located —for a murder—hello!—that's that ninety horse-power Despard that was stolen from Murdock the other day, or I'll eat my hat."

He had raised the hood and was straining his eyes to catch a glimpse of the maker's number on the engine, which had been all but obliterated by a few judicious blows of a hammer.

Garrick was busy telling McBirney also about the marks of the tire on the floor, as the detective looked over one car after another, as if he had unearthed a veritable treasure-trove.

"No, your man could not have been at either of the gambling joints," agreed McBirney, as Garrick finished, "or he wouldn't have called up. But he must have known them intimately. Perhaps he was in the pay of someone there."

McBirney was much interested in what had been discovered, and was trying to piece it together with what we had known before. "I wonder whether he's the short fellow who drove the car when it was seen up there, or the big fellow who was in the car when Warrington was shot, up-state?"

The question was, as yet, unanswerable. None of us had been able to catch a glimpse of his figure, muffled, in the darkness

Arthur B. Reeve

when he shot us.

All we knew was that even this man was unidentified and at large. The murderer, desperate as he was, was still free and unknown, too. Were they one and the same? What might not either one do next?

We sat down in one of the stolen cars and held a midnight council of war. There were four of us, and that meant four different plans. Dillon was for immediate and wholesale arrests. McBirney was certain of one thing. He would claim the cars he could identify. The garage people could not help knowing now that we had been there, and we conceded the point to him with little argument, though it took great tact on Garrick's part to swing over Dillon.

"I'm for arresting the garage-keeper, whoever he proves to be," persisted Dillon, however.

"It won't do any good," objected Garrick.

"Don't you see that it will be better to accept his story, or rather seem to, and then watch him?"

"Watch him?" I asked, eager to propose my own plan of waiting there and seizing each person who presented himself. "How can you watch one of these fellows? They are as slippery as eels,—and as silent as a muffler," I added, taking good-humouredly the general laugh that greeted my mixed metaphor.

"You've suggested the precise idea, Marshall, by your very objection," broke in Garrick, who up to this time had been silent as to his own plan.

"I've a brand-new system of espionage. Trust it to me, and you can all have your way."

CHAPTER XII

THE DETECTAPHONE

I found it difficult to share Garrick's optimism, however. It seemed to me that again the best laid plans of one that I had come to consider among the cleverest of men had been defeated, and it is not pleasant to be defeated, even temporarily. But Garrick was certainly not discouraged.

As he had said at the start, it was no ordinary criminal with whom we had to deal. That was clear. There had been gunmen and gangmen in New York for years, we knew, but this fellow seemed to be the last word, with his liquid bullets, his anesthetic shells and his stupefying gun.

We had agreed that the garage keeper would, of course, shed little light on the mystery. He was a crook. But he would find no difficulty, doubtless, in showing that there was nothing on which to hold him.

Still, Garrick had evidently figured out a way to go ahead while we had all been floundering around, helpless. His silence had merely masked his consideration of a plan.

"You three stay here," he ordered. "If anyone should come in, hold him. Don't let anyone get away. But I don't think there will be anyone. I'll be back within an hour or so."

It was far past midnight already, as we sat uncomfortably in the reeking atmosphere of the garage. The hours seemed to drag interminably. Almost I wished that something would happen to break the monotony and the suspense. Our lonely vigil went unrewarded, however. No one came; there was not even a ring at the telephone.

As nearly as I could figure it out, McBirney was the only one who seemed to have gained much so far. He had looked over the cars most carefully. There were half a dozen of them, in all.

"I don't doubt," he concluded, "that all of them have been stolen. But there are only two here that I can identify. They certainly are clever at fixing them up. Look at all the parts they keep ready for use. They could build a car, here."

"Yes," agreed Dillon, looking at the expensive "junk" that was lying about. "There is quite enough to warrant closing the place, only I suppose Garrick is right. That would defeat our own purpose."

At last Garrick returned from his hurried trip down to the office. I don't know what it was we expected him to bring, but I think we were more or less disappointed when it proved to be merely a simple oblong oak box with a handle.

He opened it and we could see that it contained in reality nothing but a couple of ordinary dry cells, and some other paraphernalia. There were two black discs, attached to a metal headpiece, discs about two and a half inches in diameter, with a circular hole in the centre of each, perhaps an inch across, showing inside what looked like a piece of iron or steel.

Garrick carefully tested the batteries with a little ammeter which he carried in a case.

"Sixteen amperes," he remarked to himself, "I don't attempt to use the batteries when they fall below five. These are all right."

From a case he took a little round black disc, about the same size as the other two. In its face it had a dozen or so small holes perforated and arranged in the shape of a six-pointed star.

"I wonder where I can stow this away so that it won't attract attention?" he asked.

Garrick looked about for the least used part of the garage and decided that it was the back. Near the barred window lay a pile of worn tires which looked as if it had been seldom disturbed except to be added to. When one got tires as cheaply as the users of this garage did, it was folly to bother much about the repair of old ones.

Back of this pile, then, he threw the little black disc carelessly, only making sure that it was concealed. That was not difficult, for it was not much larger than a watch in size.

To it, I noticed, he had attached two plugs that were "fool-proof"—that is, one small and the other large, so that they could not be inserted into the wrong holes. A long flexible green silk covered wire, or rather two wires together, led from the disc. By carefully moving the tires so as to preserve the rough appearance they had of being thrown down hastily into the discard, he was able to conceal this wire, also, in such a way as to bring it secretly to the barred window and through it.

Next he turned his attention to the telephone itself. Another instrument which he had brought with him was inserted in place of the ordinary transmitter. It looked like it and had evidently been prepared with that in view. I assumed that it must act like the ordinary transmitter also, although it must have other uses as well. It was more of a job to trace out the course of the telephone wires and run in a sort of tap line at a point where it would not be likely to be noted. This was done by Garrick, still working in silence, and the wires from it led behind various things until they, too, reached another window and so went to the outside.

As Garrick finished his mysterious tinkering and rose from his dusty job to brush off his clothes, he remarked, "There, now you may have your heart's desire, Dillon, if all you want to do is to watch these fellows."

"What is it?" I hastened to ask, looking curiously at the oak box which contained still everything except the tiny black disc and the wires leading out of the window from it and from the new telephone transmitter.

"This little instrument," he answered slowly, "is much more sensitive, I think, than any mechanical or electrical eavesdropper that has ever been employed before. It is the detectaphone—a new unseen listener."

"The detectaphone?" repeated Dillon. "How does it work?"

"Well, for instance," explained Garrick, "that attachment which I placed on the telephone is much more than a sensitive transmitter such as you are accustomed to use. It is a form of that black disc which you saw me hide behind the pile of tires. There are, in both, innumerable of the minutest globules of carbon which are floating around, as it were, making it alive at all times to every sound vibration and extremely sensitive even to the slightest sound waves. In the case of the detectaphone transmitter, it only replaces the regular telephone transmitter and its presence will never be suspected. It operates just as well when the receiver is hung up as when it is off the hook, as far as the purpose I have in mind is concerned, as you shall see soon. I have put both forms in so that even if they find the one back of the tires, even the most suspicious person would not think that anything was contained in the telephone itself. We are dealing with clever people and two anchors to windward are better than one."

Dillon nodded approval, but by the look on his face it was evident that he did not understand the whole thing yet.

"That other disc, back of the tires," went on Garrick, "is the ordinary detective form. All that we need now is to find a place to install this receiving box—all this stuff that is left over—the two batteries, the earpieces. You see the whole thing is very compact. I can get it down to six inches square and four inches thick, or I can have it arranged with earpieces so that at least six people can 'listen in' at once—forms that can be used in detective work to meet all sorts of conditions. Then there is another form of the thing, in a box about four inches square and, perhaps, nine or ten inches long which I may bring up later for another purpose when we find out what we are going to do with the ends of those wires that are now dangling on the outside of the window. We must pick up the connection in some safe and inconspicuous place outside the garage."

The window through which the wires passed seemed to open, as I had already noticed, on a little yard not much larger than a court. Garrick opened the window and stuck his head out as far as the iron bars would permit. He sniffed. The odor was anything but pleasant. It was a combination of "gas" from the garage and stale beer from the saloon.

"No doubt about it, that is a saloon," remarked Garrick, "and they must pile empty kegs out there in the yard. Let's take a walk around the corner and see what the front of the place looks like."

It was a two and a half story building, with a sloping tin roof, of an archaic architecture, in a state of terrible decay and dilapidation, and quite in keeping with the neighbourhood. Nevertheless a bright gilt sign over a side door read, "Hotel Entrance."

"I think we can get in there to-morrow on some pretext," decided Garrick after our inspection of the "Old Tavern," as the crazy letters, all askew, on one of the windows denoted the place. "The Old Tavern looks as if it might let lodgings to respectable gentlemen—if they were roughly enough dressed. We can get ourselves up as a couple of teamsters and when we get in that will give us a chance to pick up the ends of those wires to-morrow. That will be time enough, I'm sure, and it is the best we can do, anyhow."

We returned from our walk around the block to the garage where Dillon and McBirney were waiting for us.

"I leave you free to do what you please, Dillon," answered Garrick to the commissioner's inquiry, "as long as you don't pinch this place which promises to be a veritable gold-mine. McBirney, I know, will reduce the number of cars here tomorrow by at least two. But don't, for heaven's sake, let out any suspicion about those things I have just hidden here. And now, as for me, I'm going uptown and get a few hours' sleep."

Dillon and McBirney followed, leaving us, shortly, to get a

couple of men from the nearest police station to see that none of the cars were taken out before morning.

We rode up to our apartment, where a message was awaiting us, telling that Warrington had passed a very good day and was making much more rapid progress than even Dr. Mead had dared hope. I could not help wondering how much was due to the mere tonic presence daily of Violet Winslow.

I had a sound sleep, although it was a short one. Garrick had me up early, and, by digging back in his closet, unearthed the oldest clothes he had. We improved them by sundry smears of dirt in such a way that when we did start forth, no one would have accused us of being other than we were prepared to represent ourselves—workmen who had been laid off from a job on account of bad business conditions. We decided to say that we were seeking another position.

"How do I look?" I asked seriously, for this was serious business to me.

"I don't know whether to give you a meal ticket, or to call a cop when I look at you, Marshall," laughed Garrick.

"Well, I feel a good deal safer in this rig than I did last night, in this part of the city," I replied as we hopped off a surface car not far from our destination. "I almost begin to feel my part. Did you see the old gink with the gold watch on the car? If he was here I believe I'd hold him up, just to see what it is like. I suppose we are going to apply for lodgings at the famous hostelry, the Old Tavern?"

"I had that intention," replied Garrick who could see no humour in the situation, now that we were on the scene of action. "The place looks even more sordid in daylight than at night. Besides, it smells worse."

Arthur B. Reeve

We entered the tavern, and were greeted with a general air of rough curiosity, which was quickly dispelled by our spending ten cents, and getting change for a bill. At least we were good for anything reasonable, and doubts on that score settled by the man behind the bar, he consented to enter into conversation, which ultimately resulted in our hiring a large back room upstairs in the secluded caravansary which supplied "Furnished Rooms for Gentlemen Only."

Garrick said that we would bring our things later, and we went upstairs. We were no sooner settled than he was at work. He had brought a rope ladder, and, after fastening it securely to the window ledge, he let himself down carefully into the narrow court below.

That was the only part of the operation that seemed to be attended with any risk of discovery and it was accomplished safely. For one thing the dirt on the windows both of the garage and the tavern was so thick that I doubt whether so much caution was really necessary. Nevertheless, it was a relief when he secured the ends of the wires from the detectaphone and brought them up, pulling in the rope ladder after him.

It was now the work of but a minute to attach one of the wires that led from the watchcase disc back of the pile of tires to the oak box with its two storage batteries. Garrick held the ear-pieces, one to each ear, then shoved them over his head, in place.

"It works—it works," he cried, with as much delight as if he had not been positive all along that it would.

"Here, try it yourself," he added, taking the headgear off and handing the receivers to me.

I put the black discs at my ears, with the little round holes over the ear openings. It was marvellous. I could hear the men washing down one of the cars, the swash of water, and, best of all, the low-toned, gruff gossip.

"Just a couple of the men there, now," explained Garrick. "I gather that they are talking about what happened last night. I heard one of them say that someone they call 'the Chief' was there last night and that another man, 'the Boss,' gave him orders to tell no one outside about it. I suppose the Chief is our friend with the stupefying gun. The Boss must be the fellow who runs the garage. What are they saying now? They were grumbling about their work when I handed the thing over to you."

I listened, fascinated by the marvel of the thing. I could hear perfectly, although the men must have been in the front of the garage.

"Well, there's two of them yer won't haveter wash no more," one man was saying. "A feller from the perlice come an' copped off two—that sixty tin can and the ninety Despard."

"Huh—so the bulls are after him?"

"Yeh. One was here all night after the fight."

"Did they follow the Chief?"

"Follow the Chief? Say, when anyone follows the Chief he's gotter be better than any bull that ever pounded a beat."

"What did the Boss say when he heard it?"

"Mad as—. We gotter lay low now."

"The Chief's gone up-state, I guess."

"We can guess all we want. The Boss knows. I don't."

"Why didn't they make a pinch? Ain't there nobody watchin' now?"

"Naw. They ain't got nothin' on us. Say, the Chief can put them fellers just where he wants 'em. See the paper this morning? That was some raid up at the joint—eh?"

"You bet. That Garrick's a pretty smooth chap. But the Chief can put it all over him."

"Yep," agreed the other speaker.

I handed the receivers back to Garrick with a smile.

"You are not without some admirers," I remarked, repeating the conversation substantially to him. "They'd shoot up the neighbourhood, I imagine, if they knew the truth."

Hour after hour we took turns listening at the detectaphone. We gathered a choice collection of slang and epithets, but very little real news. However, it was evident that they had a wholesome respect for both the Chief and the Boss. It seemed that the real head of the gang, if it was a gang, had disappeared, as one of the men had already hinted "up-state."

Garrick had meanwhile brought out the other detectaphone box, which was longer and larger than the oak box.

"This isn't a regular detactaphone," he explained, "but it may vary the monotony of listening in and sometime I may find occasion to use it in another way, too."

In one of the long faces were two square holes, from the edges of which the inside walls focussed back on two smaller, circular diaphragms. That made the two openings act somewhat like megaphone horns to still further magnify the sound which was emitted directly from this receiver without using any earpieces, and could be listened to anywhere in the room, if we chose. This was attached to the secret arrangement that had been connected with the telephone by replacing the regular by the prepared transmitter.

One of us was in the room listening all the time. I remember once, while Guy had gone uptown for a short time, that I heard the telephone bell ring in the device at my ear. Out of the larger box issued a voice talking to one of the men.

It was the man whom they referred to as the Chief. He had nothing to say when he learned that the Boss had not showed up since early morning after he had been quizzed by the police. But he left word that he would call up again.

"At least I know that our gunman friend, the Chief, is going to call up to-night," I reported to Garrick on his return.

"I think he'll be here, all right," commented Garrick. "I called up Dillon while I was out and he was convinced that the best way was, as I said, to seem to let up on them. They didn't get a word out of the fellow they call the Boss. He lives down here a couple of streets, I believe, in a pretty tough place, even worse than the Old Tavern. I let Dillon get a man in there, but I haven't much hope. He's only a tool of the other whom they call Chief. By the way, Forbes has disappeared. I can't find a trace of him since the raid on the gambling joint."

"Any word from Warrington?" I asked.

"Yes, he's getting along finely," answered Guy mechanically, as if his thoughts were far away from Warrington. "Queer about Forbes," he murmured, then cut himself short. "And, oh," he added, "I forgot to tell you that speaking about Forbes reminds me that Herman has been running out a clew on the Rena Taylor case. He has been all over the country up there, he reports to Dillon, and he says he thinks the car was seen making for Pennsylvania.

"They have a peculiar license law there, you know—at least he says so—that enables one to conceal a car pretty well. Much good that does us."

"Yes," I agreed, "you can always depend on a man like Herman to come along with something like that—"

Just then the "master station" detectaphone connected with the telephone in the garage began to talk and I cut myself short. We seemed now at last about to learn something really important. It was a new voice that said, "Hello!"

"Evidently the Boss has come in without making any noise," remarked Guy. "I certainly heard no one through the other instrument. I fancy he was waiting for it to get dark before coming around. Listen."

It was a long distance call from the man they called Chief. Where he was we had no means of finding out, but we soon found out where he was going.

"Hello, Boss," we heard come out of the detectaphone box.

"Hello, Chief. You surely got us nearly pinched last night. What was the trouble?"

"Oh, nothing much. Somehow or other they must have got on to us. I guess it was when I called up the joint on Forty-eighth Street. Three men surprised me, but fortunately I was ready. If they hadn't stopped at the door before they opened it, they might have got me. I put 'em all out with that gun, though. Say, I want you to help me on a little job that I am planning.

"Yes? Is it a safe one? Don't you think we'd better keep quiet for a little while?"

"But this won't keep quiet. Listen. You know I told you about writing that letter regarding Warrington to Miss Winslow, when I was so sore over the report that he was going to close up the Forty-eighth Street joint, right on top of finding that Rena Taylor had the 'goods' on the Forty-seventh Street place? Well, I was a fool. You said so, and I was,"

"You were—that's right."

"I know it, but I was mad. I hadn't got all I wanted out of those places. Well, anyhow, I want that letter back—that's all. It's bad to have evidence like that lying around. Why, if they ever get a real handwriting expert they might get wise to something from that handwriting, I'm afraid. I must have been crazy to do it that way."

"What became of the letter?"

"She took it to that fellow Garrick and I happen to know that Warrington that night, after leaving Garrick, went to his apartment and put something into the safe he has there. Oh, Warrington has it, all right. What I want to do is to get that letter back while he is laid up near Tuxedo. It isn't much of a safe, I understand. I think a can opener would do the job. We can make the thing look like a regular robbery by a couple of yeggs. Are you on?"

"No, I don't get you, Chief."

"Why?"

"It's too risky."

"Too risky?"

"Yes. That fellow Garrick is just as likely as not to be nosing around up there. I'd go but for that."

"I know. But suppose we find that he isn't there, that he isn't in the house—has been there and left it. That would be safe enough. You're right. Nothing doing if he's there. We must can him in some way. But, say,—I know how to get in all right without being seen. I'll tell you later. Come on, be a sport. We won't try it if anybody's there. Besides, if we succeed it will help to throw a scare into Warrington."

The man on our end of the telephone appeared to hesitate.

"I'll tell you what I'll do, Chief," he said at length. "I'll meet you at the same place as we met the other day—you know where I mean—some time after twelve. We'll talk it over. You're sure about the letter?"

"As sure as if I'd seen it."

"All right. Now, be there. I won't promise about this Warrington business. We'll talk that over. But I have other things I want to tell you—about this situation here at the garage. I want to know how to act."

"All right. I'll be there. Good-bye."

"So long, Chief."

The conversation stopped. I looked anxiously at Garrick to see how he had taken it.

"And so," he remarked simply, as after a moment's waiting we made sure that the machine had stopped talking, "it appears that our friends, the enemy, are watching us as closely as we are watching them—with the advantage that they know us and we don't know them, except this garage fellow."

Garrick lapsed into silence. I was rapidly turning over in my mind what we had just overheard and trying to plan some way of checkmating their next move.

"Here's a plot hatching to rob Warrington's safe," I exclaimed helplessly.

"Yes," repeated Garrick slowly, "and if we are going to do anything about it, it must be done immediately, before we arouse suspicion and scare them off. Did you hear those footsteps over the detectaphone? That was the Boss going out of the garage. So, they expect me around there, nosing about Warrington's apartment. Well, if I do go there, and then ostentatiously go away again, that will lure them on."

He reached his decision quickly. Grabbing his hat, he led the way out of the Old Tavern and up the street until we came to a drug store with a telephone.

I heard him first talking with Warrington, getting from him the combination of the safe, over long distance. Then he called up his office and asked the boy to meet him at the Grand Central subway station with a package, the location of which he described minutely.

"We'll beat them to it," he remarked joyously, as we started leisurely uptown to meet the boy.

Arthur B. Reeve

CHAPTER XIII

THE INCENDIARY

"The Warrington estate owns another large apartment house, besides the one where Warrington has his quarters, on the next street," remarked Garrick, half an hour later, after we had met the boy from his office. "I have arranged that we can get in there and use one of the empty suites."

Garrick had secured two rather good-sized boxes from the boy, and was carrying them rather carefully, as if they contained some very delicate mechanism.

Warrington, we found, occupied a suite in a large apartment on Seventy-second Street, and, as we entered, Garrick stopped and whispered a few words to the hall-boy.

The boy seemed to be more than usually intelligent and had evidently been told over the telephone by Warrington that we were coming. At least we had no trouble, so far.

Warrington's suite was very tastefully furnished for bachelor quarters. In the apartment, Garrick unwrapped one of the packages, and laid it open on the table, while he busied himself opening the safe, using the combination that Warrington had given him.

I waited nervously, for we could not be sure that no one had got ahead of us, already. There was no need for anxiety, however.

"Here's the letter, just as Warrington left it," reported Garrick in a few minutes, with some satisfaction, as he banged the safe door shut and restored things so that it would not look as though the little strong box had been touched.

Meanwhile, I had been looking curiously at the box on the table. It did not seem to be like anything we had ever used before. One end was open, and the lid lifted up on a pair of hinges. I lifted it and looked in. About half way down the box from the open end was a partition which looked almost as if some one had taken the end of the box and had just shoved it in, until it reached the middle.

The open half was empty, but in the other half I saw a sort of plate of some substance covering the outside of the shoved-in end. There was also a dry cell and several arrangements for adjustments which I did not understand. Back of the whole thing was a piece of mechanism, a clockwork interrupter, as I learned later. Wires led out from the closed end of the box.

Garrick shoved the precious letter into his pocket and then placed the box in a corner, where it was hidden by a pile of books, with the open end facing the room in the direction of the antiquated safe. The wires from the box were quickly disposed of and dropped out of the window to the yard, several stories below, where we could pick them up later as we had done with the detectaphone.

"What's that?" I asked curiously, when at last he had finished and I felt at liberty to question him.

"Well, you see," he explained, "there is no way of knowing yet just how the apartment will be entered. They apparently have some way, though, which they wouldn't discuss over the telephone. But it is certain that as long as they know that there is anyone up here, they will put off the attempt. They said that."

He was busily engaged restoring everything in the room as far as possible to its former position.

"My scheme," he went on, "is for us now to leave the apartment ostentatiously. I think that is calculated to insure the burglary, for they must have someone watching by this time. Then we can get back to that empty apartment in the house on the next street, and before they can get around to start anything, we shall be prepared for them."

Garrick stopped to speak to the hall-boy again as we left, carrying the other box. What he said I did not hear but the boy nodded intelligently.

After a turn down the street, a ride in a surface car for a few blocks and back again, he was satisfied that no one was following us and we made our way into the vacant apartment on Seventy-third Street, without being observed.

Picking up the wires from the back yard of Warrington's and running them across the back fence where he attached them to other wires dropped down from the vacant apartment was accomplished easily, but it all took time, and time was precious, just now.

In the darkness of the vacant room he uncovered and adjusted the other box, connected one set of wires to those we had led in and another set to an apparatus which looked precisely like the receiver of a wireless telegraph, fitting over the head with an earpiece. He placed the earpiece in position and began regulating the mechanism of the queer looking box.

"I didn't want to use the detectaphone again," he explained as he worked, "because we haven't any assurance that they'll talk, or, if they do, that it will be worth while to listen. Besides, there may be only one of them."

"Then what is this?" I asked.

"Well," he argued, "they certainly can't work without light of some kind, can they?"

I acquiesced.

"This is an instrument which literally makes light audible," he pursued.

"Hear light?" I repeated, in amazement.

"Exactly," he reiterated. "You've said it. It was invented to assist the blind, but I think I'll be able to show that it can be used to assist justice—which is blind sometimes, they say. It is the optophone."

He paused to adjust the thing more accurately and I looked at it with an added respect.

"It was invented," he resumed, "by Professor Fournier d'Albe, a lecturer on physics at the University of Birmingham, England, and has been shown before many learned societies over there."

"You mean it enables the blind to see by hearing?" I asked.

Arthur B. Reeve

"That's it," he nodded. "It actually enables the blind to locate many things, purely by the light reflected by them. Its action is based on the peculiar property of selenium, which, you probably know, changes its electrical conductivity under the influence of light. Selenium in the dark is a poor conductor of electricity; in the light it, strange to say, becomes a good conductor. Variations of light can thus be transmuted into variations of sound. That pushed-in end of the box which we hid over in Warrington's had, as you might have noticed, a selenium plate on the inside partition, facing the open end of the box."

"I understand," I agreed, vaguely.

"Now," he went on, "this property of selenium is used for producing or rather allowing to be transmitted an electric current which is interrupted by a special clockwork interrupter, and so is made audible in this wireless telephone receiver which I have here connected with this second box. The eye is replaced by the ear as the detector of light—that is all."

It might have been all, but it was quite wonderful to me, even if he spoke of it so simply. He continued to adjust the thing as he talked.

"The clockwork has been wound up by means of a small handle, and I have moved that rod along a slit until I heard a purring sound. Then I moved it until the purring sound became as faint as possible. The instrument is at the present moment in its most sensitive state."

"What does it sound like?" I asked.

"Well, the passage of a hand or other object across the aperture is indicated by a sort of murmuring sound," he replied, "the loudest sound indicating the passage of the edges where the contrast is greatest. In a fairly bright light, even the swiftest shadow is discoverable. Prolonged exposure, however, blinds the optophone, just as it blinds the eye."

"Do you hear anything now?" I asked watching his face curiously.

"No. When I turned the current on at first I heard a ticking or rasping sound. I silenced that. But any change in the amount of light in that dark room over there would restore the sound, and its intensity would indicate the power of the light."

He continued to listen.

"When I first tried this, I found that a glimpse out of the window in daylight sounded like a cinematograph reeling off a film. The ticking sank almost into silence as the receiving apparatus was held in the shadow of the office table, and leaped into a lively rattle again when I brought it near an electric-light bulb. I blindfolded myself and moved a piece of blotting paper between the receiver and the light. I could actually hear the grating of the shadow, yes, I heard the shadow pass. At night, too, I have found that it is even affected by the light of the stars."

He glanced out of the window in the direction of Warrington's, which we could not see, however, since it was around an angle of the building.

"See," he went on, "the moon is rising, and in a few minutes, I calculate, it will shine right into that room over there on Seventy-second Street. By using this optophone, I could tell you the moment it does. Try the thing, yourself, Tom."

I did so. Though my ear was untrained to distinguish

between sounds I could hear just the faintest noise.

Suddenly there came a weird racket. Hastily I looked up at Garrick in surprise.

"What is that?" I asked endeavouring to describe it. "Are they there now?"

"No," he laughed. "That was the moon shining in. I wanted you to hear what a difference it makes. When a ray of the sun, for instance, strikes that 'feeler' over there, a harmonious and majestic sound like the echo of a huge orchestra is heard. The light of the moon, on the other hand, produces a different sound—lamenting, almost like the groans of the wounded on a battlefield."

"So you can distinguish between various kinds of light?"

"Yes. Electric light, you would find if anyone came in and switched it on over there, produces a most unpleasant sound, sometimes like two pieces of glass rubbed against each other, sometimes like the tittering laugh of ghosts, and I have heard it like the piercing cry of an animal. Gaslight is sobbing and whispering, grating and ticking, according to its intensity. By far the most melodious and pleasing sound is produced by an ordinary wax candle. It sounds just like an aeolian harp on which the chords of a solemn tune are struck. I have even tried a glow-worm and it sounded like a bee buzzing. The light from a red-hot piece of iron gives the shrillest and most ear-splitting cry imaginable."

He took the receiver back from me and adjusted it to his own ear.

"Yes," he confirmed, "that was the moon, as I thought. It's a peculiar sound. Once you have heard it you're not likely to forget it. I must silence the machine to that."

We had waited patiently for a long time, and still there was no evidence that anyone had entered the room.

"I'm afraid they decided not to attempt it after all," I said, finally.

"I don't think so," replied Garrick. "I took particular pains to make it seem that the road was clear. You remember, I spoke to the hall-boy twice, and we lingered about long enough when we left. It isn't much after midnight. I wonder how it was that they expected to get in. Ah—there goes the moon. I can hear it getting fainter all the time."

Suddenly Garrick's face was all animation. "What is it?" I asked breathlessly.

"Someone has entered the room. There is a light which sounds just like an electric flashlight which is being moved about. They haven't switched on the electric light. Now, if I were sufficiently expert I think I could tell by the varying sounds at just what that fellow is flashing the light. There, something passed directly between the light and the box. Yes, there must be two of them—that was the shadow of a human being, all right. They are over in the corner by the safe, now. The fellow with the flashlight is bending down. I can tell, because the other fellow walked between the light and the box and the light must be held very low, for I heard the shadows of both of his legs."

Garrick was apparently waiting only until the intruders, whoever they were, were busily engaged in their search before he gave the alarm and hurried over in an attempt to head off their escape by their secret means of entrance.

"Tom," he cried, as he listened attentively, "call up the apartment over there and get that hall-boy. Tell him he must not run that elevator up until we get there. No one must leave or enter the building. Tell him to lock the front door and conceal himself in the door that leads down to the cellar. I will ring the night bell five times to let him know when to let us in."

I was telephoning excitedly Garrick's instructions and as he waited for me to finish he was taking a last turn at the optophone before we made our dash on Warrington's.

A suppressed exclamation escaped him. I turned toward him quickly from the telephone and hung up the receiver.

"What's the matter?" I asked anxiously.

For a moment he did not reply, but seemed to be listening with an intensity that I knew betokened something unexpected.

"Tom," he cried abruptly, stripping the receiver from his head with a jerk and clapping it over my own ears, "quick!— tell me what you hear. What does it sound like to you? What is it? I can't be mistaken."

I listened feverishly. Not having had a former acquaintance with the machine, I did not know just what to make of it. But from the receiver of the little optophone there seemed to issue the most peculiar noise I had ever heard a mechanical instrument make.

It was like a hoarse rumbling cry, now soft and almost plaintive, again louder and like a shriek of a damned soul in the fires of the nether world. Then it died down, only to spring up again, worse than before.

If I had been listening to real sounds instead of to light I should have been convinced that the thing was recording a murder.

I described it as best I could. The fact was that the thing almost frightened me by its weird novelty.

"Yes—yes," agreed Garrick, as the sensations I experienced seemed to coincide with his own. "Exactly what I heard myself. I felt sure that I could not be mistaken. Quick, Tom,—get central on that wire!"

A moment later he seized the telephone from me. I had expected him to summon the police to assist us in capturing two crooks who had, perhaps, devised some odd and scientific method of blowing up a safe.

"Hello, hello!" he shouted frantically over the wire. "The fire department! This is eight hundred Seventy-second—on the corner; yes, yes—northeast. I want to turn in an alarm. Yes—quick! There is a fire—a bad one—incendiary—top floor. No, no—I'm not there. I can see it. Hurry!"

Arthur B. Reeve

CHAPTER XIV

THE ESCAPE

He had dropped the telephone receiver without waiting to replace it on the hook and was now dashing madly out of the empty apartment and down the street.

The hall-boy at Warrington's had done exactly as I had ordered him. There was the elevator waiting as Garrick gave the five short rings at the nightbell and the outside door was unlocked. No one had yet discovered the fire which we knew was now raging on the top floor of the apartment.

We were whirled up there swiftly, just as we heard echoing through the hall and the elevator shaft from someone who had an apartment on the same floor the shrill cry of, "Fire, fire!"

Tenants all the way up were now beginning to throw open their doors and run breathlessly about in various states of undress. The elevator bell was jangling insistently.

In the face of the crisis the elevator boy looked at Garrick appealingly.

"Run your car up and down until all are out who want to go," ordered Garrick. "Only tell them all that an alarm has already been turned in and that there is no danger except to the suite that is on fire. You may leave us here."

We had reached the top floor and stepped out. I realised fully now what had happened. Either the robbers had found out only too quickly that they had been duped or else they had reasoned that the letter they sought had been hidden in a place in the apartment for which they had no time to hunt.

It had probably been the latter idea which they had had and, instead of hunting further, they had taken a quicker and more unscrupulous method than Garrick had imagined and had set the room on fire. Fortunately that had been promptly and faithfully reported to us over the optophone in time to localize the damage.

"At least we were able to turn in an alarm only a few seconds after they started the fire," panted Garrick, as he strained to burst in the door.

Together we managed to push it in, and rushed into the stifle of Warrington's suite. The whole thing was in flames and it was impossible for us to remain there longer than to take in the situation.

Accordingly we retreated slowly before the fierce blaze. One of the other tenants came running with a fire extinguisher in either hand from wall rack down the hall on this floor. As well try to drown a blast furnace. They made no impression whatever.

Personally I had expected nothing like this. I had been prepared up to the time the optophone reported the fire to dash over and fight it out at close quarters with two as desperate and resourceful men as underworld conditions in

New York at that time had created. Instead we saw no one at all.

The robbers had evidently worked in seconds instead of minutes, realizing that they must take no risks in a show-down with Garrick. Rooms that might perhaps have given some clew of their presence, perhaps finger-prints which might have settled their identity at once, were now being destroyed. We had defeated them. We had the precious letter. But they had again slipped away.

Firemen were now arriving. A hose had been run up, and a solid stream of water was now hissing on the fire. Smoke and steam were everywhere as the men hacked and cut their way at the very heart of the hungry red monster.

"We are only in the way here, Tom," remarked Garrick, retreating finally. "Our friends must have entered and escaped by the roof. There is no other way."

He had dashed up ahead of the firemen. I followed. Sure enough, the door out on the roof had been broken into. A rope tied around a chimney showed how they had pulled themselves up and later let themselves down to the roof of the next apartment some fifteen feet lower. We could see an open door leading to the roof there, which must also have been broken open. That had evidently been the secret method of which the Chief had spoken to the Boss, whoever they might be, who bore these epithets.

Pursuit was useless, now. All was excitement. From the street we could hear the clang of engines and trucks arriving and taking their positions, almost as if the fire department had laid out the campaign beforehand for this very fire.

Anyone who had waited a moment or so in the other

apartment down the street might have gone downstairs without attracting any attention. Then he might have disappeared in or mingled with the very crowd on the street which he had caused to gather. Late as it was, the crowd seemed to spring from nowhere, and to grow momentarily as it had done during the raid on the gambling joint. It was one of the many interesting night phenomena of New York.

What had been intended to be one of the worst fires and to injure a valuable property of the Warrington estate had, thanks to the prompt action of Garrick, been quickly turned into only a minor affair, at the worst. The fire had eaten its way into two other rooms of Warrington's own suite, but there it had been stopped. The building itself was nearly fireproof, and each suite was a unit so that, to all intents and purposes, it might burn out without injury to others.

Still, it was interesting to watch the skill and intuition of the smoke-eaters as they took in the situation and almost instantly seemed to be able to cope with it.

Sudden and well-planned though the incendiary assault had been, it was not many minutes before it was completely under control. Men in rubber coats and boots were soon tramping through the water-soaked rooms of Warrington. Windows were cracked open and the air in the rooms was clearing.

We followed in cautiously after one of the firemen. Everywhere was the penetrating smell of burnt wood and cloth. In the corner was the safe, still hot and steaming. It had stood the strain. But it showed marks of having been tampered with.

"Somebody used a 'can-opener' on it," commented Garrick, looking at it critically and then ruefully at the charred wreck of his optophone that had tumbled in the ashes of the pile of books under which it had been hidden, "Yes, that was the scheme they must have evolved after their midnight conference,—a robbery masked by a fire to cover the trail, and perhaps destroy it altogether."

"If we had only known that," I agreed, "we might have saved what little there was in that safe for Warrington. But I guess he didn't keep much there."

"No," answered Garrick, "I don't think he did. All I saw was some personal letters and a few things he apparently liked to have around here. I suppose all the really valuable stuff he has was in a safety-deposit vault somewhere. There was a packet of—it's gone! What do you think of that?" he exclaimed looking up from the safe to me in surprise.

"Packet of what?" I asked. "What is gone?"

"Why," replied Garrick, "I couldn't help noticing it when I opened the safe before, but Warrington had evidently saved every line and scrap of writing that Violet Winslow had ever given him and it was all in one of the compartments of the safe. The compartment is empty!"

Neither of us could say a word. What reason might there be why anyone should want Warrington's love letters? Was it to learn something that might be used to embarrass him? Might it be for the purpose of holding him up for money? Did the robber want them for himself or was he employed by another? These and a score of other questions flashed, unanswered, through my mind.

"I wonder who this fellow is that they call the Chief?" I ventured at last.

"I can't say—yet," admitted Garrick. "But he's the cleverest I have ever met. His pace is rapid, but I think we are getting up with it, at last. There's no use sticking around here any longer, though. The place for us, I think, is downtown, getting an earful at the other end of that detectaphone."

The engines and other apparatus were rolling away from the fire when we regained the street and things were settling themselves down to normal again.

We rode downtown on the subway, and I was surprised when Garrick, instead of going all the way down to the crosstown line that would take us to the Old Tavern, got off at Forty-second Street.

"What's the idea of this?" I asked.

"Do you think I'm going to travel around the city with that letter in my pocket?" he asked. "Not much, since they seem to set such a value on getting it back. Of course, they don't know that I have it. But they might suspect it. At any rate I'm not going to run any chances of losing it."

He had stopped at a well-known hotel where he knew the night clerk. There he made the letter into a little package, sealed it, and deposited it in the safe.

"Why do you leave it here?" I asked.

"If I go near the office, they might think I left it there, and I certainly won't leave it in my own apartment. They may or may not suspect that I have it. At any rate, I'd hate to risk meeting them down in their own region. But here we are not followed. I can leave it safely and to-morrow I'll get it and deposit it in a really safe place. Now, just to cover up my tracks, I'm going to call up Dillon, but I'm going up

Arthur B. Reeve

Broadway a bit before I do so, so that even he will not know I've been in this hotel. I think he ought to know what has happened to-day."

"What did he say?" I asked as Garrick rejoined me from the telephone booth, his face wearing a scowl of perplexity.

"Why, he knew about it already," replied Garrick. "I got him at his home. Herman, it seems, got back from some wild-goose chase over in New Jersey and saw the report in the records filed at police headquarters and telephoned him."

"Herman is one of the brightest detectives I ever met," I commented in disgust. "He always manages to get in just after everybody else. Has he any more news?"

"About the car?" asked Garrick absently. "Nothing except that he ran down the Pennsylvania report and found there was nothing in it. Now he says that he thinks the car may have returned to New York, perhaps by way of Staten Island, for he doubts whether it could have slipped in by New Jersey."

"Clever," I ejaculated. "I suppose that occurred to him as soon as he read about the fire. I have to hand it to him for being a deducer."

Garrick smiled.

"There's one thing, though, he does know," he added, "and that is the gossip of the underworld right here in New York."

"I should hope so," I replied. "That was his business to know. Why, has he found out anything really new?"

"Why—er—yes. Dillon tells me that it now appears that

Forbes had been intimate with that Rena Taylor."

"Yes?" I repeated, not surprised.

"At least that's what Herman has told him."

"Well," I exclaimed in disgust, "Forbes is a fine one to run around with stool-pigeons and women of the Tenderloin, in addition to his other accomplishments, and then expect to associate with a girl like Violet Winslow."

"It is scandalous," he agreed. "Why, according to Dillon and Herman, she must have been getting a good deal of evidence through her intimacy with Forbes. They probably gambled together, drank together, and—"

"Do you suppose Forbes ever found out that she was really using him?"

Garrick shook his head. "I can't say," he replied. "There isn't much value in this deductive, long distance detective work. You reason a thing out to your satisfaction and then one little fact knocks all your clever reasoning sky-high. The trouble here is that on this aspect of the case the truth seems to have been known by only two persons—and one of them is dead, while the other has disappeared."

"Strange what has become of Forbes," I ruminated.

"It is indeed," agreed Garrick. "But then he was such a night-hawk that anything might easily have happened and no one be the wiser. Since you saw him enter the gambling joint the night of the raid, I've been unable to get a line on him. He must have gone through the tunnel to the ladies' poolroom, but after he left that, presumably, I can't find a trace of him. Where he went no one seems to know. This bit of gossip that

Herman has unearthed is the first thing I've heard of him, definitely, for two days."

"If Rena Taylor were alive," I speculated, "I don't think you'd have to look further for Forbes than to find her."

"But she isn't alive," concluded Garrick, "and there is nothing to show that there was anyone else at the poolroom for women who interested him—and—well, this isn't getting back to business."

He turned toward the street.

"Let's go down on a surface car," he said. "I think we ought to learn something down there at the Old Tavern, now. If these people have done nothing more, they'll think they have at least given an example of their resourcefulness and succeeded in throwing another scare into Warrington. But there's one thing I'd like to be able to tell Mr. Chief, however. He can't throw any scare into me, if that's his game."

CHAPTER XV

THE PLOT

We had been able to secure a key to the hotel entrance of the Old Tavern, so that we felt free to come and go at any hour of the day or night. We let ourselves in and mounted the stairs cautiously to our room.

"At least they haven't discovered anything, yet," Garrick congratulated himself, looking about, as I struck a light, and finding everything as we had left it.

Late as it was, he picked up the detective receiver of the mechanical eavesdropper and held it to his ears, listening intently several moments.

"There's someone in the garage, all right," he exclaimed. "I can hear sounds as if he were moving about among the cars. It must be the garage keeper himself—the one they call the Boss. I don't think our clever Chief would have the temerity to show up here yet, even at this hour."

We waited some time, but not the sound of a voice came from the instrument.

"It would be just like them to discover one of these

Arthur B. Reeve

detectaphones," remarked Garrick at length. "This is a good opportunity. I believe I'll just let myself down there in the yard again and separate those two wires, further. There's no use in risking all the eggs in one basket."

While I listened in, Garrick cautiously got out the rope ladder and descended. Through the detectaphone I could hear the noise of the man walking about the garage and was ready at the window to give Garrick the first alarm of danger if he approached the back of the shop, but nothing happened and he succeeded in accomplishing his purpose of further hiding the two wires and returning safely. Then we resumed listening in relays.

It was early in the morning when there came a telephone call to the garage and the garage keeper answered it.

"Where did you go afterward?" he asked of the man who was calling him.

Garrick had quickly shifted to the instrument by which we could overhear what was said over the telephone.

A voice which I recognised instantly as that of the man they called the Chief replied, "Oh, I had a little business to attend to—you understand. Say, they got that fire out pretty quickly, didn't they? How do you suppose the alarm could have been turned in so soon?"

"I don't know. But they tell me that Garrick and that other fellow with him showed up, double quick. He must have been wise to something."

"Yes. Do you know, I've been thinking about that ever since. Ever hear of a little thing called a detectaphone? No? Well, it's a little arrangement that can be concealed almost anywhere. I've been wondering whether there might not be one hidden about your garage. He might have put one in that night, you know. I'm sure he knows more about us than he has any right to know. Hunt around there, will you, and see if you can find anything?"

"Hold the wire."

We could hear the Boss poking around in corners, back of the piles of accessories, back of the gasoline tank, lifting things up and looking under them, apparently flashing his light everywhere so that nothing could escape him.

A hasty exclamation was recorded faithfully over our detectaphone, close to the transmitter, evidently.

"What the deuce is this?" growled a voice.

Then over the telephone we could hear the Boss talking.

"There's a round black thing back of a pile of tires, with a wire connected to it. One side of it is full of little round holes. Is that one of those things?"

"Yes," came back the voice, "that's it." Then excitedly, "Smash it! Cut the wires—no, wait—look and see where they run. I thought you'd find something. Curse me for a fool for not thinking of that before."

Garrick had quickly himself detached the wire from the receiving instrument in our room and, sticking his head cautiously out of the window, he swung the cut ends as far as he could in the direction of a big iron-shuttered warehouse down the street in the opposite direction from us.

Then he closed the window softly and pulled down the

switch on the other detectaphone connected with the fake telephone receiver.

He smiled quietly at me. The thing worked still. We had one connection left with the garage, anyway.

There was a noise of something being shattered to bits. It was the black disc back of the pile of tires. We could hear the Boss muttering to himself.

"Say," he reported back over the telephone, "I've smashed the thing, all right, and cut the wires, too. They ran out of the back window to that mercantile warehouse, down the street, I think. I'll look after that in the morning. It's so dark over there now I can't see a thing."

"Good!" exclaimed the other voice with satisfaction. "Now we can talk. That fellow Garrick isn't such a wise guy, after all. I tell you, Boss, I'm going to throw a good scare into them this time—one that will stick."

"What is it?"

"Well, I got Warrington, didn't I?"

"Yes."

"You know I can't always be following that fellow, Garrick. He's too clever at dodging shadows. Besides, unless we give him something else to think about he may get a line on one of us,—on me. Don't you understand? Warrington's out of it for the present. I saw to that. Now, the thing is to fix up something to call them off, altogether, something that we can use to hold them up."

"Yes—go on—what?"

"Why—how about Violet Winslow?"

My heart actually skipped beating for a second or two as I realised the boldness and desperation of the plan.

"What do you mean—a robbery up there in Tuxedo?"

"No, no, no. What good would a robbery do? I mean to get her—kidnap her. I guess Warrington would call the whole thing off to release her—eh?"

"Say, Chief, that's going it pretty strong. I'd rather break in up there and leave a threat of some kind, something that would frighten them. But, this,—I'm afraid—"

"Afraid—nothing. I tell you, we've got to do it. They're getting too close to us. We've either got to get Garrick or do something that'll call him off for good. Why, man, the whole game is up if he keeps on the way he has been going—let alone the risk we have of getting caught."

The Boss seemed to be considering.

"How will you get a chance to do it?" he asked at length.

"Oh, I'll get a chance, all right. I'll make a chance," came back the self-confident reply.

It sent a shiver through me merely to contemplate what might happen if Violet Winslow fell into such hands. Mentally I blessed Garrick for his forethought in having the phony 'phone in the garage against possible discovery of the detective instrument.

"You know this poisoned needle stuff that's been in the papers?" pursued the Chief.

"Bunk—all bunk," came back the Boss promptly.

"Is that so?" returned the Chief. "Well, you're right about it as far as what has been in the papers is concerned. I don't know but I doubt about ninety-nine and ninety-nine hundredths per cent of it, too. But, I'll tell you,—it can be done. Take it from me—it can be done. I've got one of the best little sleepmakers you ever saw—right from Paris, too. There, what do you know about that?"

I glanced hastily, in alarm, at Garrick. His face was set in hard lines, as he listened.

"Sleepmaker—Paris," I heard him mutter under his breath, and just a flicker of a smile crossed the set lines of his fine face.

"Yes, sir," pursued the voice of the Chief, "I can pull one of those poisoned needle cases off and I'm going to do it, if I get half a chance."

"When would you do it?" asked the Boss, weakening.

"As soon as I can. I've a scheme. I'm not going to tell you over the wire, though. Leave it to me. I'm going up to our place, where I left the car. I'll study the situation out, up there. Maybe I'll run over and look over the ground, see how she spends her time and all that sort of thing. I've got to reckon in with that aunt, too. She's a Tartar. I'll let you know. In the meantime, I want you to watch that place on Forty-seventh Street. Tell me if they make any move against it. Don't waste any time, either. I can't be out of touch with things the way I was the last time I went away. You see, they almost put one across on us—in fact they did put one across with that detectaphone thing. Now, we can't let that happen again. Just keep me posted, see?"

They had finished talking and that was apparently all we were to get that night, or rather that morning, by way of warning of their plot for the worst move yet.

It was enough. If they would murder and burn, what would they stop at in order to strike at us through the innocent figure of Violet Winslow? What might not happen to such a delicate slip of a girl in the power of such men?

"At least," rapped out Garrick, himself smothering his alarm, "they can't do anything immediately. It gives us time to prepare and warn. Besides, before that we may have them rounded up. The time has come for something desperate. I won't be trifled with any longer. This last proposal goes just over the limit."

As for me, I was speechless. The events of the past two days, the almost sleepless nights had sapped my energy. Even Garrick, though he was a perfect glutton for work, felt the strain.

It was very late, or rather very early, and we determined to snatch a few moments of sleep at the Old Tavern before the rest of the world awoke to the new day. It was only a couple of hours that we could spare, but it was absolutely necessary.

In spite of our fatigue, we were up again early and after another try at the phony 'phone which told us that only the men were working in the garage, we were on our way up to Garrick's apartment.

We had scarcely entered when the telephone boy called up to say that there was a Mr. Warrington on long distance trying to get us. Garrick eagerly asked to have him put on our wire.

Warrington, it seemed, had been informed of the fire by one

of his agents and was inquiring anxiously for details, especially about the letter. Garrick quickly apologised for not calling up himself, and relieved his anxiety by assuring him that the letter was safe.

"And how are you?" he asked of Warrington.

"Convalescing rapidly," laughed back the patient, to whom the loss of anything was a mere bagatelle beside the letter. Garrick had not told him yet of the stealing of the other letters. "Getting along fine,—thanks to a new tonic which Dr. Mead has prescribed for me."

"I can guess what it is."

Warrington laughed again. "Yes—I've been allowed to take short motor trips with Violet," he explained.

The natural manner in which "Violet" replaced "Miss Winslow" indicated that the trips had not been without result.

"Say, Warrington," burst out Garrick, seeing an opportunity of introducing the latest news, "I hate to butt in, but if you'll take my advice, you'll just cut out those trips a few days. I don't want to alarm you unnecessarily, but after to-day I want Miss Winslow never to be out of sight of friends—friends, I said; not one, but several."

"Why—what's the matter?" demanded Warrington in alarm.

"I can't explain it all over the telephone," replied Garrick, sketching out hastily something of what we had overheard. "I'll try to see you before long—perhaps to-day. Don't forget. I want you to warn Miss Winslow yourself. You can't put it too strongly. Use your judgment about Mrs. de Lancey. I don't want to get you in wrong with her. But, remember, it's a matter of life or death—or perhaps worse. Try to do it without unnecessarily alarming Miss Winslow, if you can. Just fix it up as quietly as possible. But be positive about it. No, I can't explain more over the wire now. But—no more outings for either of you, and particularly Miss Winslow, until I raise the ban."

Warrington had been inclined to argue the matter at first, but Garrick of course quickly prevailed, the more so because Warrington realised that in his condition he was anything but an adequate body-guard for her if something unexpected should happen.

"Oh—I had a call the other day," reported Warrington as an afterthought before hanging up the receiver. "It was from McBirney. He says one of his unofficial scouts has told him of seeing a car that might have been mine up this way lately."

Garrick acquiesced to the information which, to us, was not new. "Yes," he said, "there have been several such reports. And, by the way, that reminds me of something. You will have to put at our disposal one of your cars down here."

"Go as far as you like. What do you want—a racer?"

"Why—yes, if it's in perfect condition. You see, we may have to do some unexpected sleuthing in it."

"Go as far as you like," repeated Warrington, now thoroughly aroused by the latest development of the case. "Spare nothing, Garrick—nothing. Curse my luck for being laid up! Every dollar I have is at your disposal, Garrick, to protect her from those scoundrels—damn them!"

"Trust me, Warrington," called back Garrick. "I give you my

word that it's my fight now."

"Garrick—you're a brick," came back Warrington as the conversation closed.

"Good heavens, Guy," I exclaimed when he hung up the receiver after calling up Warrington's garage and finding out what cars were available, "Are we going to have to extend operations over the whole State, after all?"

"We may have to do almost anything," he replied, "if our scientific murderer tries some of his smooth kidnapping tricks. It's possible that McBirney may be right about that car being up there. Certainly we know that it has been up there, whether it is now or not."

"And Herman wrong about its being in the city?" I suggested. "Well, one guess is as good as another in a case like this, I suppose."

It had been a great relief to get back to our rooms and live even for a few minutes like civilised beings. I suggested that we might have a real breakfast once more.

I could tell, however, that Garrick's mind was far away from the thought of eating, and that he realised that a keen, perhaps the keenest, test of his ability lay ahead of him, if he was to come out successfully and protect Violet Winslow in the final battle with the scientific gunman. I did not interrupt him.

CHAPTER XVI

THE POISONED NEEDLE

Over a still untasted grapefruit Garrick was considering what his next move should be. As for me, even this temporary return to a normal life caused me to view things in a different light.

There had been, as the Chief and the Boss had hinted at in their conversation, a wave of hysteria which had swept over the city only a short time before regarding what had come to be called the "poisoned needle" cases. Personally I had doubted them and I had known many doctors and scientists as well as vice and graft investigators who had scouted them, too.

"Garrick," I said at length, "do you really think that we have to deal with anything in this case but just plain attempted kidnapping of the old style?"

He shook his head doubtfully. I knew him to be anything but an alarmist and waited impatiently for him to speak.

"I wouldn't think so," he said at length slowly, "except for one thing."

"What's that?" I asked eagerly.

"His mention of the 'sleepmakers' and Paris," he replied briefly.

Garrick had risen and walked over to a cabinet in the corner of his room. When he returned it was with something gleaming in the morning sunshine as he rolled it back and forth on a piece of paper, just a shining particle. He picked it up carefully.

I bent over to look at it more closely and there, in Garrick's hand, was a tiny bit of steel, scarcely three-eighths of an inch long, a mere speck. It was like nothing of which I had ever heard or read. Yet Garrick himself seemed to regard the minute thing with a sort of awe. As for me, I knew not what to make of it. I wondered whether it might not be some new peril.

"What is it?" I asked at length, seeing that Garrick might be disposed to talk, if I prompted him.

"Well," he answered laconically, holding it up to the light so that I could see that it was in reality a very minute, pointed hollow tube, "what would you say if I told you it was the point of a new—er—poisoned needle?"

He said it in such a simple tone that I reacted from it toward my own preconceived notions of the hysterical newspaper stories.

"I've heard about all the poisoned needle stories," I returned. "I've investigated some of them and written about them for my paper, Guy. And I must say still that I doubt them. Now in the first place, the mere insertion of a hypodermic needle—of course, you've had it done, Guy—is something so painful that anyone in his senses would cry aloud. Then to administer a drug that way requires a great deal of skill and knowledge of anatomy, if it is to be done with full and quick effect."

Garrick said nothing, but continued to regard the hollow point which he had obtained somewhere, perhaps on a previous case.

"Why, such an injection," I continued, recalling the result of my former careful investigations on the subject, "couldn't act instantaneously anyhow, as it must if they are to get away with it. After the needle is inserted, the plunger has to be pushed down, and the whole thing would take at least thirty seconds. And then, the action of the drug. That would take time, too. It seems to me that in no case could it be done without the person's being instantly aware of it and, before lapsing into unconsciousness, calling for help or—"

"On the contrary," interrupted Garrick quietly, "it is absurdly easy. Waiving the question whether they might not be able to get Violet Winslow in such a situation where even the old hypodermic method which you know would serve as well as any other, why, Marshall, just the hint that fellow dropped tells me that he could walk up to her on the street or anywhere else, and—"

He did not finish the sentence, but left it to my imagination. It was my turn, now, to remain silent.

"You are right, though, Tom, in one respect," he resumed a moment later. "It is not easy by the old methods that everyone now knows. For instance, take the use of chloral-knock-out drops, you know. That is crude, too. Hypodermics and knock-out drops may answer well enough, perhaps, for the criminals whose victims are found in cafes and dives of a low order. But for the operations of an aristocratic criminal of to-day—and our friend the Chief seems to belong to the aristocracy of the underworld—far more subtle methods are required. Let me show you something."

Carefully, from the back of a drawer in the cabinet, where it was concealed in a false partition, he pulled out a little case. He opened it, and in it displayed a number of tiny globes and tubes of thin glass, each with a liquid in it, some lozenges, some bonbons, and several cigars and cigarettes.

"I'm doing this," he remarked, "to show you, Tom, that I'm not unduly magnifying the danger that surrounds Violet Winslow, after hearing what I did over that detectaphone. Perhaps it didn't impress you, but I think I know something of what we're up against."

From another part of the case he drew a peculiar looking affair and handed to me without a word. It consisted of a glass syringe about two inches long, fitted with a glass plunger and an asbestos washer. On the other end of the tube was a hollow point, about three-eighths of an inch long—just a shiny little bit of steel such as he had already showed me.

I looked at it curiously and, in spite of my former assurance, began to wonder whether, after all, the possibility of a girl being struck down suddenly, without warning, in a public place and robbed—or worse—might not take on the guise of ghastly reality.

"What do you make of it?" asked Garrick, evidently now enjoying the puzzled look on my face.

I could merely shrug my shoulders.

"Well," he drawled, "that is a weapon they hinted at last

night. The possibilities of it are terrifying. Why, it could easily be plunged through a fur coat, without breaking."

He took the needle and made an imaginary lunge at me.

"When people tell you that the hypodermic needle cannot be employed in a case like this that they are planning," he continued, "they are thinking of ordinary hypodermics. Those things wouldn't be very successful usually, anyhow, under such circumstances. But this is different. The very form of this needle makes it particularly effective for anyone who wishes to use it for crime. For instance—take it on a railroad or steamship or in a hotel. Draw back the plunger—so—one quick jab—then drop it on the floor and grind it under your heel. The glass is splintered into a thousand bits. All evidence of guilt is destroyed, unless someone is looking for it practically with a microscope."

"Yes," I persisted, "that is all right—but the pain and the moments before the drug begins to work?"

With one hand Garrick reached into the case, selecting a little thin glass tube, and with the other he pulled out his handkerchief.

"Smell that!" he exclaimed, bending over me so that I could see every move and be prepared for it.

Yet it was done so quickly that I could not protect myself.

"Ugh!" I ejaculated in surprise, as Garrick manipulated the thing with a legerdemain swiftness that quite baffled me, even though he had given me warning to expect something.

Everyone has seen freak moving picture films where the actor suddenly bobs up in another place, without visibly crossing the intervening space. The next thing I knew, Garrick was standing across the room, in just that way. The handkerchief was folded up and in his pocket.

It couldn't have been done possibly in less than a minute. What had happened? Where had that minute or so gone? I felt a sickening sensation.

"Smell it again?" Garrick laughed, taking a step toward me.

I put up my hand and shook my head negatively, slowly comprehending.

"You mean to tell me," I gasped, "that I was—out?"

"I could have jabbed a dozen needles into you and you would never have known it," asserted Garrick with a quiet smile playing over his face.

"What is the stuff?" I asked, quite taken aback.

"Kelene—ethyl chloride. Whiff!—and you are off almost in a second. It is an anaesthetic of nearly unbelievable volatility. It comes in little hermetically sealed tubes, with a tiny capillary orifice, to prevent its too rapid vaporising, even when opened for use. Such a tube may be held in the palm of the hand and the end crushed off. The warmth of the hand alone is sufficient to start a veritable spray. It acts violently on the senses, too. But kelene anaesthesia lasts only a minute or so. The fraction of time is long enough. Then comes the jab with the real needle—perhaps another whiff of kelene to give the injection a chance. In two or three minutes the injection itself is working and the victim is unconscious, without a murmur—perhaps, as in your case, without any clear idea of how it all happened—even without recollection of a handkerchief, unable to recall any sharp pain of a needle or anything else."

He was holding up a little bottle in which was a thick, colorless syrup.

"And what is that?" I asked, properly tamed and no longer disposed to be disputatious.

"Hyoscine."

"Is it powerful?"

"One one-hundredth of a grain of this strength, perhaps less, will render a person unconscious," replied Garrick. "The first symptom is faintness; the pupils of the eyes dilate; speech is lost; vitality seems to be floating away, and the victim lapses into unconsciousness. It is derived from henbane, among ether things, and is a rapid, energetic alkaloid, more rapid than chloral and morphine. And, preceded by a whiff of kelene, not even the sensations I have described are remembered."

I could only stare at the outfit before me, speechless.

"In Paris, where I got this," continued Garrick, "they call these people who use it, 'endormeurs'—sleepmakers. That must have been what the Chief meant when he used that word. I knew it."

"Sleepmakers," I repeated in horror at the very idea of such a thing being attempted on a young girl like Violet Winslow.

"Yes. The standard equipment of such a criminal consists of these little thin glass globes, a tiny glass hypodermic syringe with a sharp steel point, doped cigars and cigarettes. They use various derivatives of opium, like morphine and heroin, also codeine, dionin, narcein, ethyl chloride and bromide, nitrite of amyl, amylin,—and the skill that they have acquired in the manipulation of these powerful drugs stamps them as the most dangerous coterie of criminals in existence. Now," he concluded, "doubt it or not, we have to deal with a man who is a proficient student of these sleepmakers. Who is he, where is he, and when will he strike?"

Garrick was now pacing excitedly up and down the room.

"You see," he added, "the police of Europe by their new scientific methods are driving such criminals out of the various countries. Thank heaven, I am now prepared to meet them if they come to America."

"Then you think this is a foreigner?" I asked meekly.

"I didn't say so," Garrick replied. "No. I think this is a criminal exceptionally wide awake, one who studies and adopts what he sees whenever he wants it. If you recall, I warned you to have a wholesome respect for this man at the very start, when we were looking at that empty cartridge."

I could restrain my admiration of him no longer. "Guy," I exclaimed, heartily, astounded by what I had seen, "you—you are a wonder!"

"No," he laughed, "not wonderful, Tom,—only very ordinary. I've had a chance to learn some things abroad, fortunately. I've taken the time to show you all this because I want you to appreciate what it is we are up against in this case of Violet Winslow. You can understand now why I was so particular about instructing Warrington not to let her go anywhere unattended by friends. There's nothing inherently impossible in these poisoned needle stories—given the right conjunction of circumstances. What we have to guard against principally is letting her get into any situation where the circumstances make such a thing possible. I've almost a notion to let the New York end of this case go altogether for a while and take a run up to Tuxedo to warn her and Mrs. de Lancey personally. Still, I think I put it strongly enough with Warrington so that—"

Our telephone tinkled insistently.

"Hello," answered Garrick. "Yes, this is Garrick. Who is this? Warrington? In Tuxedo? Why, my dear boy, you needn't have gone personally. Are you sure you're strong enough for such exertion? What—what's that? Warrington—it—it isn't—not to New York?"

Garrick's face was actually pale as he fairly started back from the telephone and caught my eye.

"Tom," he exclaimed huskily to me, "Violet Winslow left for New York on the early train this morning!"

I felt my heart skip a beat, then pound away like a sledge-hammer at my ribs as the terrible possibilities of the situation were seared into my brain.

"Yes, Warrington—a letter to her? Read it—quick," I heard Garrick's tense voice repeating. "I see. Her maid Lucille was taken very ill a few days ago and she allowed her to go to her brother who lives on Ninth Street. I understand. Now—the letter."

I could not hear what was said over the telephone, but later Garrick repeated it to me and I afterwards saw the letter itself which I may as well reproduce here. It said:

"Since I left you, mademoiselle, I am very ill here at the

home of my brother. I have a nice room in the back of the house on the first floor and now that I am getting better I can sit up and look out of the window."

"I am very ill yet, but the worst is past and some time when you are in New York I wish I could see you. You have always been so good to me, mademoiselle, that I hope I may soon be back again, if you have not a maid better than your poor Lucille."

"Your faithful servant,

"LUCILLE DE VEAU."

"And she's already in the city?" asked Garrick of Warrington as he finished reading the letter. "Mrs. de Lancey has gone with her—to do some shopping. I see. That will take all day, she said? She is going to call on Lucille—to-night—that's what she told her new maid there? To-night? That's all right, my boy. I just wanted to be sure. Don't worry. We'll look out for her here, all right. Now, Warrington, you just keep perfectly quiet. No relapses, you know, old fellow. We can take care of everything. I'm glad you told me. Good-bye."

Garrick had finished up his conversation with Warrington in a confident and reassuring tone, quite the opposite to that with which he had started and even more in contrast with the expression on his face as he talked.

"I didn't want to alarm the boy unnecessarily," he explained to me, as he hung up the receiver. "I could tell that he was very weak yet and that the trip up to Tuxedo had almost done him up. It seems that she thought a good deal of Lucille— there's the address—99 Ninth. You can never tell about these maids, though. Lucille may be all right—or the other maid may be all bad, or vice versa. There's no telling. The worst of it is that she and her aunt are somewhere in the city, perhaps shopping. It only needs that they become separated for something, anything, to happen. There's been no time to warn her, either, and she's just as likely to visit that Lucille to-night alone as not. Gad—I'm glad I didn't fly off up there to Tuxedo, after all. She'll need someone here to protect her."

Garrick was considering hastily what was to be done. Quickly he mapped out his course of action.

"Come, Tom," he said hurriedly to me, as he wrapped up a little cedar box which he took from the cabinet where he kept the endormeur outfit. "Come—let's investigate that Ninth Street address while we have time."

CHAPTER XVII

THE NEWSPAPER FAKE

Within a few minutes we were sauntering with enforced leisure along Ninth Street, in a rather sordid part, inhabited largely, I made out, by a slightly better class of foreigners than some other sections of the West Side.

As we walked along, I felt Garrick tugging at my arm.

"Slow up a bit," he whispered under his breath. "There's the house which was mentioned in the maid's note."

It was an old three-story brownstone building with an entrance two or three steps up from the sidewalk level. Once, no doubt, it had housed people of some means, but the change in the character of the neighbourhood with shifting population had evidently brought it to the low estate where it now sheltered one family on each floor, if not more. At least that was the general impression one got from a glance at the cheapened air of the block.

Garrick passed the house so as not to attract any attention, and a little further on paused before an apartment house, not of the modern elevator construction, but still of quiet and decent appearance. At least there were no children spilling out from its steps into the street, in imminent danger of their young lives from every passing automobile, as there were in the tenements of the block below.

He entered the front door which happened to be unlatched and we had no trouble in mounting the stairs to the roof.

What he intended doing I had no idea yet, but he went ahead with assurance and I followed, equally confident, for he must have had adventures something like this before. On the roof, a clothesline, which he commandeered and tied about a chimney, served to let him down the few feet from the higher apartment roof to that of the dwelling house next to it, one of the row in which number 99 was situated.

Quickly he tiptoed over to the chimney of the brownstone house a few doors down and, as he did so, I saw him take from his pocket the cedar box. A string tied to a weight told him which of the flues reached down to the room on the first floor, back.

That determined, he let the little cedar box fastened to an entwined pair of wires down the flue. He then ran the wires back across the roof to the apartment, up, and into a little storm shed at the top of the last flight of stairs which led from the upper hall to the roof.

"There is nothing more that we can do here just yet," he remarked after he had hauled himself back to me on the higher roof. "We are lucky not to have been disturbed, but if we stay here we are likely to be observed."

Cautiously we retraced our steps and were again on the street without having alarmed any of the tenants of the flat through which we had gained access to the roofs.

It was now the forenoon and, although Garrick instituted a search in every place that he could think of where Mrs. de Laacey and Violet Winslow might go, including the homes of those of their friends whose names we could learn, it was without result. I don't think there can be many searches more hopeless than to try to find someone in New York when one has no idea where to look. Only chance could possibly have thrown them in our way and chance did not favour us.

There was nothing to do but wait for the time when Miss Winslow might, of her own accord, turn up to visit her former maid for whom she apparently had a high regard.

Inquiries as to the antecedents of Lucille De Veau were decidedly unsatisfactory, not that they gave her a bad character, but because there simply seemed to be nothing that we could find out. The maid seemed to be absolutely unknown. Her brother was a waiter, though where he worked we could not find out, for he seemed to be one of those who are constantly shifting their positions.

Garrick had notified Dillon of what he had discovered, in a general way, and had asked him to detail some men to conduct the search secretly for Miss Winslow and her aunt, but without any better results than we had obtained. Apparently the department stores had swallowed them up for the time being and we could only wait impatiently, trusting that all would turn out right in the end. Still, I could not help having some forebodings in the matter.

It was in the middle of the afternoon that we had gone downtown to Garrick's office, after stopping to secure the letter from the safe in the uptown hotel where it had been deposited for security during the night and placing it in a safety deposit vault where Garrick kept some of his own valuables. Garrick had selected his office as a vantage point to which any news of Miss Winslow and her aunt might be sent by those whom we had out searching. No word came, however, and the hours of suspense seemed to drag interminably.

"You're pretty well acquainted on the STAR?" Garrick asked me at last, after we had been sitting in a sort of mournful silence wondering whether those on the other side might not be stealing a march on us.

"Why, yes, I know several people there," I replied. "Why do you ask?"

"I was just thinking of a possible plan of campaign that might be mapped out to bring these people from under cover," he remarked thoughtfully. "Do you think you could carry part of it through?"

I said I would try and Garrick proceeded to unfold a scheme which he had been revolving all day. It consisted of as ingenious a "plant" as I could well imagine.

"You see," he outlined, "if you could go over to the Star office and get them to run off a few copies of the paper, after they are through with the regular editions, I believe we can get the Chief started and then all we should have to do would be to follow him up—or someone who would lead us to him."

The "plant," in short, consisted in writing a long and circumstantial story of the discovery of new evidence against the ladies' poolroom, which so far had been scarcely mentioned in the case. As Garrick laid it out, the story was to tell of a young gambler who was said to be in touch with the district attorney, in preference to saying the police.

In fact, his idea was to write up the whole gambling situation as we knew it on lines that he suggested. Then a "fake" edition of the paper was to be run off, bearing our story on the front page. Only a few copies were to be printed, and they were to be delivered to us. The thing had been done before by detectives, I knew, and in this case Warrington was to foot the bill, which might prove to be considerable.

At least it offered me some outlet for my energies during the rest of the afternoon when the failure to receive any reports about the two women whom we were seeking began to wear on my nerves.

It took some time to arrange the thing with those in authority on the Star, but at last that was done and I hastened back to Garrick at his office to tell him that all that remained to do was the actual writing of the story.

Garrick had just finished testing an arrangement in a large case, almost the size of a suitcase, and had stood it in a corner, ready to be picked up and carried off the instant there was any need for it. There was still no word of Miss Winslow and Mrs. de Lancey and it began to look as if we should not hear from them until Violet Winslow turned up on her visit to her former maid.

Together we plunged into the preparation of the story, the writing of which fell to me while Garrick now and then threw in a suggestion or a word of criticism to make it sound stronger for his purpose. Thus the rest of the afternoon passed in getting the thing down "pat."

I flatter myself that it was not such a bad piece of work when we got through with it. By dint of using such expressions as "It is said," "It is rumoured," "The report about the Criminal Courts Building is," "An informant high in the police department," and crediting much to a mythical "gambler who is operating quietly uptown," we managed to tell some amazing facts.

The fake story began:

"Since the raid by the police on the luxurious gambling house in Forty-eighth Street, a remarkable new phase of sporting life has been unfolded to the District Attorney, who is quietly gathering evidence against another place situated in the same district.

"A former gambler who frequented the raided place has put many incriminating facts about the second place in the hands of the authorities who are contemplating an exposure that will stir even New York, accustomed as it is to such startling revelations. It involves one of the cleverest and most astute criminals who ever operated in this city."

"This place, which is under observation, is one which has brought tragedy to many. Young women attracted by the treacherous lure of the spinning roulette wheel or the fascination of the shuffle of cards have squandered away their own and their husband's money with often tragic results, and many of them have gone even further into the moral quagmire in the hope of earning enough money to pay their losses and keep from their families the knowledge of their gambling."

"This situation, one of the high lights in the city of lights and shadows, has been evolved, according to the official informant, through the countless number of gambling resorts that have gained existence in the most fashionable parts of the city."

"The record of crime of the clever and astute individual

already mentioned is being minutely investigated, and, it is said, shows some of the most astounding facts. It runs even to murder, which was accomplished in getting rid of an informer recently in the pay of the police."

"Against those conducting the crusade every engine of the underworld has been used. The fight has been carried on bitterly, and within less than twenty-four hours arrests are promised as a result of confessions already in the hands of the authorities and being secretly and widely investigated by them before the final blow is delivered simultaneously, both in the city and in a town up-state where the criminal believes himself unknown and secure."

There was more of the stuff, which I do not quote, describing the situation in detail and in general terms which could all have only one meaning to a person acquainted with the particular case with which we were dealing. It threw a scare, in type, as hard as could be done. I fancied that when it was read by the proper person he would be amazed that so much had, apparently, become known to the newspapers, and would begin to wonder how much more was known that was not printed.

"That ought to make someone sit up and take notice," remarked Garrick with some satisfaction, as he corrected the typewritten copy late in the afternoon. "The printing of that will take some time and I don't suppose we shall get copies until pretty late. You can take it over to the Star, Tom, and complete the arrangements. I have a little more work to do before we go up there on Ninth Street. Suppose you meet me at eight in Washington Square, near the Arch?"

CHAPTER XVIII

THE VOCAPHONE

Promptly to the dot I met Garrick at the appointed place. Not a word so far had been heard, either from Violet Winslow or Mrs. de Lancey. There was one thing encouraging about it, however. If they had become separated while shopping, as sometimes happens, we should have been likely to hear of it, at least from her aunt.

Garrick was tugging the heavy suitcase which I had seen standing ready down in his office during the afternoon, as well as a small package wrapped up in paper.

"Let me carry that suitcase," I volunteered.

We trudged along across the park, my load getting heavier at every step.

"I'm not surprised at your being winded," I panted, soon finding myself in the same condition. "What's in this—lead?"

"Something that we may need or may not," Garrick answered enigmatically, as we stopped in the shadow to rest.

He carefully took an automatic revolver from an inside

pocket and stowed it where it would be handy, in his coat.

We resumed our walk and at last had come nearly up to the house on the first floor of which the maid Lucille was. The suitcase was engaging all my attention, as I shifted it from one hand to the other. Not so Garrick, however. He was looking keenly about us.

"Gad, I must be seeing things to-night!" he exclaimed, his eyes fixed on a figure slouching along, his hat pulled down over his eyes, passing just about opposite us on the other side of the street. I looked also in the gathering dusk. The figure had something indefinably familiar about it, but a moment later it was gone, having turned the corner.

Garrick shook his head. "No," he said half to himself, "it couldn't have been. Don't stop, Tom. We mustn't do anything to rouse suspicion, now."

We came a moment later to the flat-house through the hall of which we had reached the roof that morning and in the excitement of the adventure I forgot, for the time, the mysterious figure across the street, which had attracted Garrick's attention.

Again, we managed to elude the tenants, though it was harder in the early evening than it had been in the daytime. However, we reached the roof apparently unobserved. There at least, now that it was dark, we felt comparatively safe. No one was likely to disturb us there, provided we made no noise.

Unwrapping the smaller, paper-covered package, Garrick quickly attached the wires, as he had left them, to another cedar box, like that which he had already let down the chimney up the street.

I now had a chance to examine it more closely under the light of Garrick's little electric bull's-eye. I was surprised to find that it resembled one of the instruments we had used down in the room in the Old Tavern.

It was oblong, with a sort of black disc fixed to the top. In the face of the box, just as in the other we had used, were two little square holes, with sides also of cedar, converging inward, making a pair of little quadrangular pyramidal holes which seemed to end in a small round black circle in the interior, small end.

I said nothing, but I could see that it was a new form, to all intents and purposes, of the detectaphone which we had already used.

The minutes that followed seemed like hours, as we waited, not daring to talk lest we should attract attention.

I wondered whether Miss Winslow would come after all, or, if she did, whether she would come alone.

"You're early," said a voice, softly, near us, of a sudden.

I leaped to my feet, prepared to meet anything, man or devil. Garrick seized me and pulled me down, a strong hint to be quiet. Too surprised to remonstrate, since nothing happened, I waited, breathless.

"Yes, but that is better than to be too late. Besides, we've got to watch that Garrick," said another voice. "He might be around."

Garrick chuckled.

I had noticed a peculiar metallic ring in the voices.

"Where are they?" I whispered, "On the landing below?"

Garrick laughed outright, not boisterously, but still in a way which to me was amazing in its bravado, if the tenants were really so near.

"What's this?" I asked.

"Don't you recognize it?" he answered.

"Yes," I said doubtfully. "I suppose it's like that thing we used down at the Old Tavern."

"Only more so," nodded Garrick, aloud, yet careful not to raise his voice, as before, so as not to disturb the flat dwellers below us. "A vocaphone."

"A vocaphone?" I repeated.

"Yes, the little box that hears and talks," he explained. "It does more than the detectaphone. It talks right out, you know, and it works both ways."

I began to understand his scheme.

"Those square holes in the face of it are just like the other instrument we used," Garrick went on. "They act like little megaphones to that receiver inside, you know,—magnify the sound and throw it out so that we can listen up here just as well, perhaps better than if we were down there in the room with them."

They were down there in the back room, Lucille and a man.

"Have you heard from her?" asked the man's voice, one that I did not recognise.

"Non,—but she will come. Voila, but she thought the world of her Lucille, she did. She will come."

"How do you know?"

"Because—I know."

"Oh, you women!"

"Oh, you men!"

It was evident that the two had a certain regard for each other, a sort of wild, animal affection, above, below, beyond, without the law. They seemed at least to understand each other.

Who the man was I could not guess. It was a voice that sounded familiar, yet I could not place it.

"She will come to see her Lucille," repeated the woman. "But you must not be seen."

"No—by no means."

The voice of the man was not that of a foreigner.

"Here, Lucille, take this. Only get her interested—I will do the rest—and the money is yours. See—you crush it in the handkerchief—so. Be careful—you WILL crush it before you want to use it. There. Under her nose, you know. I shall be there in a moment and finish the work. That is all you need do—with the handkerchief."

Garrick made a motion, as if to turn a switch in the little vocaphone, and rested his finger on it.

Arthur B. Reeve

"I could make those two jump out of the window with fright and surprise," he said to me, still fingering the switch impatiently. "You see, it works the other way, too, as I told you, if I choose to throw this switch. Suppose I should shout out, and they should hear, apparently coming from the fireplace, 'You are discovered. Thank you for telling me all your plans, but I am prepared for them already.' What do you suppose they would—"

Garrick stopped short.

From the vocaphone had come a sound like the ringing of a bell.

"Sh!" whispered Lucille hoarsely. "Here she comes now. Didn't I tell you? Into the next room!"

A moment later came a knock at a door and Lucille's silken rustle as she hurried to open it.

"How do you do, Lucille?" we heard a sweetly tremulous voice repeated by the faithful little vocaphone.

"Comment vous portez-vous, Mademoiselle?"

"Tres bien."

"Mademoiselle honours her poor Lucille beyond her dreams. Will you not be seated here in this easy chair?"

"My God!" exclaimed Garrick, starting back from the vocaphone. "She is there alone. Mrs. de Lancey is not with her. Oh, if we could only have prevented this!"

I had recognized, too, even in the mechanical reproduction, the voice of Violet Winslow. It came as a shock. Even though I had been expecting some such thing for hours, still the reality meant just as much, perhaps more.

Independent, self-reliant, Violet Winslow had gone alone on an act of mercy and charity, and it had taken her into a situation full of danger with her faithless maid.

At once I was alive to the situation. All the stories of kidnappings and white slavery that I had ever read rioted through my head. I felt like calling out a warning. Garrick had his finger on the switch.

"Since I have been ill, Mademoiselle, I have been doing some embroidery—handkerchiefs—are they not pretty?"

It was coming. There was not time for an instant's delay now.

Garrick quickly depressed the switch.

Clear as a bell his voice rang out.

"Miss Winslow—this is Garrick. Don't let her get that handkerchief under your nose. Out of the door—quick. Run! Call for help! I shall be with you in a minute!"

A little cry came out of the machine.

There was a moment of startled surprise in the room below. Then followed a mocking laugh.

"Ha! Ha! I thought you'd pull something like that, Garrick. I don't know where you are, but it makes no difference. There are many ways of getting out of this place and at one of them I hare a high-powered car. Violet—will go—quietly—" there were sounds of a struggle—"after the needle—"

A scream had followed immediately after a sound of shivering glass through the vocaphone. It was not Violet Winslow's scream, either.

"Like hell, she'll go," shouted a wildly familiar voice.

There was a gruff oath.

We stayed to hear no more. Garrick had already picked up the heavy suitcase and was running down the steps two at a time, with myself hard after him.

Without waiting to ring the bell at 99, he dashed the suitcase through the plate glass of the front door, reached in and turned the lock. We hurried into the back room.

Violet was lying across a divan and bending over her was Warrington.

"She—she's unconscious," he gasped, weak with the exertion of his forcible entrance into the place and carrying from the floor to the divan the lovely burden which he had found in the room. "They - they fled—two of them—the maid, Lucille—and a man I could not see."

Down the street we heard a car dashing away to the sound of its changing gears.

"She's—not—dying—is she, Garrick?" he panted bending closer over her.

Garrick bent over, too, felt the fluttering pulse, looked into her dilated eyes.

I saw him drop quickly on his knees beside the unconscious girl. He tore open the heavy suitcase and a moment later he had taken from it a sort of cap, at the end of a rubber tube, and had fastened it carefully over her beautiful, but now pale, face.

"Pump!" Garrick muttered to me, quickly showing me what to do.

I did, furiously.

"Where did you come from?" he asked of Warrington. "I thought I saw someone across the street who looked like you as we came along, but you didn't recognise us and in a moment you were gone. Keep on with that pulmotor, Tom. Thank heaven I came prepared with it!"

Eagerly I continued to supply oxygen to the girl on the divan before us.

Garrick had stooped down and picked up both the handkerchief with its crushed bits of the kelene tube and near it a shattered glass hypodermic.

"Oh, I got thinking about things, up there at Mead's," blurted out Warrington, "and I couldn't stand it. I should have gone crazy. While the doctor was out I managed to slip away and take a train to the city. I knew this address from the letter. I determined to stay around all night, if necessary. She got in before I could get to her, but I rang the bell and managed to get my foot in the door a minute later. I heard the struggle. Where were you? I heard your voice in here but you came through the front door."

Garrick did not take time to explain. He was too busy over Violet Winslow.

A feeble moan and a flutter of the eyelids told that she was coming out from the effects of the anaesthetic and the drug.

"Mortimer—Mortimer!" she moaned, half conscious. "Don't let them take me. Oh where is—"

Warrington leaned over, as Garrick removed the cap of the pulmotor, and gently raised her head on his arm.

"It's all right—Violet," he whispered, his face close to hers as his warm breath fanned her now flushed and fevered cheek.

She opened her eyes and vaguely understood as the mist cleared from her brain.

Instinctively she clung to him as he pressed his lips lightly on her forehead, in a long passionate caress.

"Get a cab, Tom," said Garrick turning his back suddenly on them and placing his hand on my shoulder as he edged me toward the hall. "It's too late to pursue that fellow, now. He's slipped through our fingers again—confound him!"

CHAPTER XIX

THE EAVESDROPPER AGAIN

It took our combined efforts now to take care not only of Violet Winslow but Warrington himself, who was on the verge of collapse after his heroic rescue of her.

I found the cab and in perhaps half an hour Miss Winslow was so far recovered that she could be taken to the hotel where she and her aunt had engaged rooms for the night.

We drew up at an unfrequented side carriage entrance of the hotel in order to avoid the eyes of the curious and Warrington jumped out to assist Violet. The strain had told on him and in spite of his desire to take care of her, he was glad to let Garrick guide him to the elevator, while I took Miss Winslow's arm to assist her.

Our first object had been to get our two invalids where they could have quiet and so regain their strength and we rode up in the elevator, unannounced, to the suite of Violet and her aunt.

"For heaven's sake—Violet—what's all this?" exclaimed Mrs. de Lancey as we four entered the room.

Arthur B. Reeve

It was the first time we had seen the redoubtable Aunt Emma. She was a large woman, well past middle age, and must have been handsome, rather than pretty, when she was younger. Everything about Mrs. de Lancey was correct, absolutely correct. Her dress looked like a form into which she had been poured, every line and curve being just as it should be, having "set" as if she had been made of reinforced concrete. In short, she was a woman of "force."

An incursion such as we made seemed to pain her correct soul acutely. And yet, I fancied that underneath the marble exterior there was a heart and that secretly she was both proud and jealous of her dainty niece.

Violet sank into a chair and Garrick deposited Warrington, thoroughly exhausted, on a couch.

Mrs. de Lancey looked sternly at Warrington, as though in some way he might be responsible. I could not help feeling that she had a peculiar sense of conscientiousness about him, that she was just a bit more strict in gauging him than she would have been if he had not been the wealthy young Mr. Warrington whom scores and hundreds of mothers and guardians in society would have welcomed for the sake of marriageable daughters no matter how black and glaring his faults. I was glad to see the way Warrington took it. He seemed to want to rest not on the merits of the Warrington blood nor the Warrington gold, but on plain Mortimer Warrington himself.

"What HAS happened, Violet?" repeated Mrs. de Lancey.

Violet had, woman-like, in spite of her condition caught the stern look that her aunt had shot at Warrington.

"Nothing, now," she replied with a note of defiance. "Lucille—

seems to have been a—a bad woman—friendly with bad men. Mr. Garrick overheard a plot to carry me off and telephoned Mortimer. Fortunately when Mortimer went up home to warn us, he found the letter and knew where I was going to-night. Ill as he was, he came all the way to the city, followed me into that house, saved me—even before Mr. Garrick could get there."

Violet's duenna was considerably mollified, though she tried hard not to admit it. Garrick seized the opportunity and poured forth a brief but connected story of what had happened.

"Well," exclaimed Mrs. de Lancey as he finished, "you children ought to be very thankful it isn't worse. Violet, I think I'll call up the house physician. You certainly need a doctor. And as for you, Mortimer,—you can't go to your apartment. Violet tells me it is all burned out. There's an empty suite across the hall. I'll telephone the room clerk and engage it for you. And you need a doctor, too. Now—there's going to be no more foolishness. You're both going to stay right here in this hotel until you're all right. Your mother and I were great friends, Mortimer, when we were girls. I—you must let me PLAY mother—for her sake."

I had been right about Mrs. de Lancey. Her voice softened and I saw a catch in Warrington's throat, too, at the mention of the mother he remembered only hazily as a small boy.

Violet and Warrington exchanged glances. I fancied the wireless said, "We've won the old lady over, at last," for Warrington continued to look at her, while she blushed a bit, then dropped her eyes to hide a happy tear.

Mrs. de Lancey was bustling about and I felt sure that in another minute every available bellhop in the hotel would be at work. As Warrington might have said in his slang, "Action is her middle name."

Garrick rose and bade our two patients a hasty good-night, tactfully forgetting to be offended by their lack of interest now in anything except each other.

"I doubt if they get much chance to be alone—not with that woman mothering them," he smiled to me, drawing me toward the door. "Don't let's spoil this chance."

Mrs. de Lancey was busy in the next room, as we stopped to say good-bye to her.

"I—I can't talk to you—now, Mr. Garrick," she cried, with a sudden, unwonted show of emotion, taking both his hands in hers. "You—you've saved my girl—there—there's nothing in this world you could have done for me—greater."

"Mrs. de Lancey," replied Garrick, deftly changing the subject, "there's just one thing. I'm afraid you are—have been, I mean,—a little hard on Mr. Warrington. He isn't what you think—"

"Mr. Garrick," she returned, in a sudden burst of confidence, "I'm afraid you, too, misunderstand me. I am not hard on the boy. But, remember. I knew his mother and father—intimately. Think of it, sir—the responsibilities that rest on that young man. Do you wonder that I—I want him better than others? Don't you see—that is why I want to hold him up to the highest standard. If Violet—marries him," she seemed to choke over the word,—"they must meet tests that ordinary people never know. Don't you understand? I've seen other young men and other young women in our circle—they were our babies once—I've seen them—go down. But I—I am proud. The Winslows, yes, and the Warringtons, they,—they SHAN'T go down—not while I have an ounce of strength or a grain of sanity. Nothing—nothing but the best that is in us—counts."

I think Mrs. de Lancey and Garrick understood each other perfectly after that. He said nothing, in fact did not need to say anything, for he looked it.

"I feel that I can safely resign my job as guardian," was all he remarked, finally. "Neither of them could be in better hands. Only, keep that boy quiet a few days. You can do it better than I can—you and Miss Winslow. Trust me to do the rest."

A moment later we were passing out through the hotel lobby, as Garrick glanced at his watch.

"A wonderful woman, after all," he mused, in the manner of one who revises an estimate formed hastily on someone else's hearsay. "Well, it's too late to do anything more to-night. I suppose those papers are printed down at the Star. We'll stop and get them in the morning. Did you recognise the voice over the vocaphone?"

"I can't say I did," I confessed.

"Perhaps you aren't used to it and things sound too metallic to you. But I did. It was the Chief."

"I suspected as much," I replied. "Where do you suppose he went?"

Garrick shrugged his shoulders.

"I doubt whether we could find him in New York to-night," he answered, slowly. "I think he must feel by this time that the town is getting too hot for him."

There was nothing that I could say, and I played the part admirably.

"Come," he decided, as he turned from the hotel in the direction, now, of our apartment. "Let's snatch a little rest. We'll need it to-morrow for the final spurt."

Tired and exhausted though I was I cannot say that I slept. At least, it may have been physical rest that I got. Certainly my mind never stopped in its dream play, as the kaleidoscopic stream of events passed before me, now in their true form, now in the fantastic shapes that constitute one of the most interesting studies of the modern psychology.

I was glad when I heard Garrick stirring in his room in the early daylight and heard him call out, "Are you awake, Tom? There are some things I want to attend to, while you drop into the Star for those papers. I'm afraid you'll have to breakfast alone. Meet me at my office as soon as you can."

He was off a few minutes later, as fresh as though he had been on a vacation instead of plunged into the fight of his life. I followed him, more leisurely, and then rode down in the infernal jam in the subway to execute his commission.

Then for an hour or two I fidgeted impatiently in his office waiting for him, until finally he came downtown in the racing car which Warrington had placed at his disposal.

He said nothing, but it was all the same to me. I had reached that nervous state where I craved something doing, as a drug-fiend craves the dope that sets his brain on fire again.

I did not ask where he was going, for I knew it intuitively, and it was not long before we were again in the part of the city where the gangster's garage was located.

We stopped and Garrick beckoned to an urchin, a couple of blocks below the garage.

"Do you want to make a dollar, kid?" he asked, jingling four quarters enticingly.

The boy's eyes never left the fist that held the tempting bait. "Betcherlife," he answered.

"Well, then," instructed Garrick, "take these newspapers. I don't want you to sell any of them on the street. But when you come to that garage over there—see it?—I want you to yell, 'Extra—special extra! All about the great gambling exposure. Warrants out!' Just go in there. They'll buy, all right. And if you say a word about anyone giving you these papers to sell—I'll chase you and get back this dollar to the last cent. You'll go to the Gerry Society—get me?"

The boy did. The bait was as alluring as the threat terrible. After Garrick had given him final instructions not to start with the papers for at least five minutes, we slipped quietly around the next street and came out near the Old Tavern, but not in front of it.

Garrick left the car—I had been riding almost on the mud guard—in charge of Warrington's man, who was to appear to be tinkering with the engine as an excuse for waiting there, and to keep an eye on anything that happened down the street.

We made our way into our room at the Tavern with more than ordinary caution, for fear that something might have been discovered. Apparently, however, the discovery of one detectaphone had been enough to disarm further suspicion, and the garage keeper had not thought it necessary to examine the telephone wires to see whether they had been tampered with in any way. The wire which he had thought led to the warehouse had seemed quite sufficient to explain everything.

In the room which we had used so much, we found the other detectaphone working splendidly. Garrick picked it up.

By the sound, evidently, someone in the garage was over-hauling a car. It may have been that they were fixing one up so that its rightful owner would never recognize it, or they may have been getting ready to take one out. There was no way of determining.

We could hear one of the workmen helping about the car, a man whom we had listened to when the instrument first introduced us to the place. The second machine, connected with the telephone, did not transmit quite as clearly as the broken detective device had done, but it served and, besides, we could both hear through this and could confirm anything that might be indistinct to either of us alone.

"The Chief has gone up-state," remarked Garrick, piecing together the conversation where we had broken into it.

"We had to hustle to make that boat," remarked a voice which I recognised as that of one of the men.

"But she got off all right, didn't she?"

"Sure—he had the tickets and everything, and her baggage had already gone aboard."

"That's Lucille, I suppose," supplied Garrick. "No doubt part of her bribe for getting Miss Winslow into their power was free passage back to France. We can't stop to take up her case, yet."

"My—but the Chief was mad," continued the voice of the man who must have been not only a machinist but a chauffeur when occasion demanded. "He had a package of letters. I don't know what they were—looked as if they might be from some woman."

"What did he do with them?" asked the Boss in a tone that showed that he knew something, at least, about them already.

"Why, he was so mad after that fellow Garrick and the other fellow beat him out, that when we went down along West Street to the boat with that other woman, he tore them up and threw them in the river."

"Did he say anything?"

"Why, I tell you he was mad. He tore 'em up and threw them in the river. I think he said there wasn't a damn thing in 'em except a lot of mush, anyhow."

An amused smile crossed Garrick's face as he added, parenthetically, "Good-bye to Warrington's love letters that they took from his safe."

"At least there has been nothing they managed to get that night of the fire that they have been able to use against Warrington," I remarked, with satisfaction.

"Listen," cautioned Garrick. "What's that they are saying? Someone has told the Boss—he's talking—that they can go over Dillon's head and get back all the gambling paraphernalia? Well, I've been there, at the raided place, to-day, and it doesn't look so. The stuff has all been taken down to headquarters. Ah, so that is the game that is in the wind, is it? Get it all back by a court order and open somewhere else. Here's our boy."

The improvised newsboy had apparently stuck his head in the door as he had been instructed, for we could hear them greet him with a growl, until he yelled lustily, "Extry, special extry! All about the big gambling exposure! Warrants out! Extry!"

"Hey, you kid," came a voice from the detectaphone, "let's see that paper. What is it—the Star? Well, I'll be—! Read that. Someone's snitched to the district attorney, I'll bet. That'll make the Chief sore, all right—and he's 'way up in the country, too. I don't dare wire it to him. No, someone'll have to take a copy of this paper up there to him and tip him off. He'll be redheaded if he doesn't know about it. He was the last time anything happened. Hurry up. Finish with this car. I'll take it myself."

Garrick laughed, almost gleefully.

"The plant has begun to work," he cried. "We'll wait here until just before he's ready to start. Three of us around our car on the street are too many. He must be getting ready for a long run."

"How much gas is there in this tank?" the gruff voice of the Boss demanded. "You dummy—not two gallons! No, you finish what you're doing. I'll fill it myself. There isn't any time for fooling now."

There was the steady trickle of the stream of gasoline as he drew it.

"Any extra tires? What! Not a new shoe in the place? Give me a couple of the best of those old ones. Never mind. Here are two over by the telephone. Say, what the devil is this wire back here - cut in on the telephone wire? Well,—rip it out! That's some more of that fellow Garrick's work. We got rid of one thing the other night. Well, thank heaven, I didn't have any telephone calls to-day. While I'm gone, you go over this place thoroughly. God knows how many other things he may have put in here."

"Confound it!" muttered Garrick, as a pair of pliers made our second detectaphone die with an expiring gasp in the middle of a sentence of profanity.

"Come on, Tom," he shouted.

There was no use now in remaining any longer in the room. Gathering up the receiving apparatus, Garrick quickly carried it down and tossed it into the waiting car around the corner. Then he sent Warrington's man to hang around, up the street, and watch what was going on at the garage.

Garrick was to drive the car himself, and we were going to leave Warrington's man behind. We could tell by the actions of the man as he stood down the street that something was taking place at the garage.

We could hear a horn blow, and I knew that the doors had opened and a big car had been backed out, slowly. Our own engine was running perfectly in spite of the seeming trouble with which we had covered up our delay. Garrick jumped in at the wheel, and I followed. The man on the corner was signalling that the car was going in the opposite direction. We leaped ahead.

As the big car ahead slipped along eastward, we followed at such a distance as not to attract attention. It was easy enough to do that, but not so easy to avoid getting tied up among the trucks laden with foodstuffs of every description which blocked the streets over in this part of town.

Where the car ahead was bound, we did not know, but I could see that the driver was a stocky fellow, who slouched down into his seat, and handled his car almost as if it had been a mere toy. It was, I felt positive, the man whom McBirney had reported one night about the neighbourhood of Longacre Square in the car which had once been Warrington's. This, at least, was a different car, I knew. Now I realised the wisdom of allowing this man, whom they called the Boss, to go free. Under the influence of Garrick's "plant," he was to lead us to the right trail to the Chief.

It was easier now to follow the car since it had worked its way into lower Fifth Avenue. On uptown it went. We hung on doggedly in the mass of traffic going north at this congested hour.

At last it turned into Forty-seventh Street. It was stopping at the ladies' gambling joint, apparently to confirm the news. I had thought that the place was closed, until the present trouble blew over, but it seemed that there must be someone there. The Boss was evidently well known, for he was immediately admitted.

Garrick did not stop. He kept on around the corner to the raided poolroom on the next street. Dillon's man, who had been stationed there to watch the place, bowed and admitted him.

"I'm going to throw it into him good, this time," remarked Garrick, as he entered. "I've been planning this stunt for an emergency—and it's here. Now for the big scare!"

CHAPTER XX

THE SPEAKING ARC

"Looks pretty deserted here," remarked Garrick to Dillon's man, who had accompanied us from the door into the now deserted gambling den.

"Yes," he grinned, "there's not much use in keeping me here since they took all the stuff to headquarters. Now and then one of the old rounders who has been out of town and hasn't heard of the raid comes in. You should see their faces change when they catch sight of my uniform. They never stop to ask questions," he chuckled. "They just beat it."

I was wondering how the police regarded Garrick's part in the matter, and while Garrick was busy I asked, "Have you seen Inspector Herman lately?"

The man laughed.

"What's the matter?" I asked, "Is he sore at having the raid pulled off over his head?"

"Sore?" the roundsman repeated, "Oh, not a bit, not a bit. He enjoyed it. It gave him so much credit," the man added sarcastically, "especially after he fell down in getting the evidence against that other place around the corner."

"Was that his case, too?" I asked.

"Sure," replied the policeman. "Didn't you know that? That Rena Taylor was working under his orders when she was killed. They tell me at headquarters he's working overtime on the case and other things connected with it. He hasn't said much, but there's someone he is after—I know. Mark my words. Herman is always most dangerous when he's quiet. The other day he was in here, said there was a man who used to be seen here a good deal in the palmy days, who had disappeared. I don't know who he was, but Herman asked me to keep a particular lookout to see if he came back for any purpose. There's someone he suspects, all right."

I wondered why the man told me. He must have seen, by the look on my face, that I was thinking that.

"I wouldn't tell it to everybody," he added confidentially, "only, most of us don't like Herman any too well. He's always trying to hog it all—gets all the credit if we pick up a clew, and,—well, most of us wouldn't be exactly disappointed to see Mr. Garrick succeed—that's all."

Garrick was calling from the back room to me, and I excused myself, while the man went back to his post at the front door. Garrick carefully closed the door into the room.

While I had been busy getting the copies of the faked edition of the Star, which had so alarmed the owner of the garage and had set things moving rapidly, Garrick had also been busy, in another direction. He had explored not only the raided gambling den, but the little back yard which ran all the way to an extension on the rear of the house in the next street, in which was situated the woman's poolroom.

He had explored, also, the caved-in tunnel enough to make absolutely certain that his suspicions had been correct in the first place, and that it ran to this other joint, from which the gamblers had made their escape. That had satisfied him, however, and he had not unearthed the remains of the tunnel or taken any action in the matter yet. Something else appeared to interest him much more at the present moment.

"I found," he said when he was sure that we were alone, "that the feed wire of the arc light that burns all the time in that main room over there in the place on Forty-seventh Street—you recall it?—runs in through the back of the house."

He was examining two wires which, from his manner, I inferred were attached to this feed wire, leading to it from the room in which we now were. What the purpose of the connection was I had no idea. Perhaps, I thought, it was designed to get new evidence against the place, though I could not guess how it was to be done. So far, except for what we had seen on our one visit, there had appeared to be no real evidence against the place, except, possibly, that which had died with the unfortunate Rena Taylor.

"What's that?" I asked, as Garrick produced a package from a closet where he had left it, earlier in the day.

I saw, after he had unwrapped it, that it was a very powerful microphone and a couple of storage cells. He attached it to the wire leading out to the electric light feed wire.

"I had provided it to be used in an emergency," he replied. "I think the time has come sooner than I anticipated."

I watched him curiously, wondering what it would be that would come next.

There followed a most amazing series of groanings and mutterings from Garrick. I could not imagine what he was up to. The whole proceeding seemed so insane that, for the moment, it left me nonplussed and speechless.

Garrick caught the puzzled look on my face.

"What's the matter?" he laughed heartily, cutting out the microphone momentarily and seeming to enjoy the joke to the utmost.

"Would you prefer to be sent to a State or a private institution?" I rasped, testily. "What insanity is all this? It sounds like the fee-faw-fum and mummery of a voodoo man."

"Come, now, Tom," he rejoined, argumentatively. "You know as well as I do what sort of people those gamblers are—superstitious as the deuce. I did this once before to-day. This is a good time to do it again, before they persuade themselves that there is nothing in that story which we printed in the Star. That fellow is in there now, probably in that room where we were, and it is possible that they may reassure him and settle his fears. Now, just suppose a murder had been committed in a room, and you knew it, and heard groanings and mutterings—from nowhere, just in the air, about you, overhead—what would you do, if you were inclined to be superstitious?"

Before I could answer, he had resumed the antics which before I had found so inexplicable.

"Cut out and run, I suppose," I replied. "But what has that to do with the case? The groanings are here—not there. You haven't been able to get in over there to attach anything, have you? What do you mean?"

"No," he admitted, "but did you ever hear what you could do with a microphone, a rheostat, and a small transformer coil if you attached them properly to a direct-current electric lighting circuit? No? Well, an amateur with a little knowledge of electricity could do it. The thing is easily constructed, and the result is a most complicated matter."

"Well?" I queried, endeavouring to follow him.

"The electric arc," he continued, "isn't always just a silent electric light. You know that. You've heard them make noises. Under the right conditions such a light can be made to talk—the 'speaking arc,' as Professor Duddell calls it. In other words, an arc light can be made to act as a telephone receiver."

I could hardly believe the thing possible, but Garrick went on explaining.

"You might call it the arcophone, I suppose. The scientific fact of the matter is that the arc is sensitive to very small variations of the current. These variations may run over a wide range of frequency. That suggested to Duddell that a direct-current arc might be used as a telephone receiver. All that you need is to add a microphone current to the main arc current. The arc reproduces sounds and speech distinctly, loud enough, even, to be heard several feet away from the light."

He had cut out the microphone again while he was talking to me. He switched it in again with the words, "Now, get ready, Tom. Just one more; then we must hurry around in that car of ours and watch the fun."

This time he was talking into the microphone. In a most solemn, sepulchral voice he repeated, "Let the slayer of Rena

Taylor beware. She will be avenged! Beware! It will be a life for a life!"

Three times he repeated it, to make sure that it would carry. Then, grabbing up his hat and coat, he dashed out of the room, past the surprised policeman at the door, and took the steps in front of the house almost at a bound.

We hardly had time to enter our own car and reach the corner of Forty-seventh Street, when the big black automobile which we had followed uptown shot by almost before the traffic man at the crossing could signal a clear road.

"We must hang onto him!" cried Garrick, turning to follow. "Did you catch a glimpse of his face? It's our man, the go-between, the keeper of the garage whom they call the Boss. He was as pale as if he had seen a ghost. I guess he did think he heard one. Between the news-paper fake and the speaking arc, I think we've got him going. There he is."

It was an exciting ride, for the man ahead was almost reckless, though he seemed to know instinctively still just when to put on bursts of speed and when to slow down to escape being arrested for speeding. We hung on, managing to keep something less than a couple of blocks behind him. It was evident that he was making for the ferry uptown across the river to New Jersey, and, taking advantage of this knowledge, Garrick was able to drop back a little, and approach the ferry by going down a different street so that there was no hint yet that we were following him.

By judicious jockeying we succeeded in getting on the boat on the opposite side from the car we were following, and in such a way that we could get off as soon as he could. We managed to cross the ferry, and, in the general scramble that attends the landing, to negotiate the hill on the other side of the river without attracting the attention of the man in the other car. His one idea seemed to be speed, and he had no suspicion, apparently, that in his flight he was being followed.

As we bowled along, forced by circumstances to take the fellow's dust, Garrick would quietly chuckle now and then to himself.

"Fancy what he must have thought," he chortled. "First the newspaper that sent him scurrying up to the gambling place for more news, or to spread the alarm, and then, while they were sitting about, perhaps while someone was talking about the strange voices they had already heard this morning, suddenly the voice from nowhere. Can you blame them if they thought it was a warning from the grave?"

Whatever actually had happened in the gambling house, the practical effect was all that even Garrick could have desired. Hour after hour, we hung to that car ahead, leaving behind the cities, and passing along the regular road through town after town.

Sometimes the road was well oiled, and we would have to drop back a bit to escape too close observation. Then we would strike a stretch where it was dry. The clouds of dust served to hide us. On we went until it was apparent that the man was now headed at least in the direction of Tuxedo.

We now passed the boundary between New York state and New Jersey and soon after that came to the house of Dr. Mead where Warrington had been convalescing until Garrick's warning had brought him, still half ill, down to the city to protect Violet Winslow. In fact, the road seemed replete with interesting reminiscences of the case, for a few miles back was the spot where Rena Taylor's body had been found, as well as the garage whence had come the rumour of the blood-stained car. There was no chance to stop and tell the surprised Dr. Mead just what had become of his patient and we had to trust that Warrington would explain his sudden disappearance himself. In fact, Garrick scarcely looked to either the right or left, so intent was he on not missing for an instant the car that was leading us in this long chase.

On we sped, around the bend where Warrington had been held up. It was a nasty curve, even in the daytime.

"I think this fellow ahead noticed the place," gritted Garrick, leaning forward. "He seemed to slow up a bit as he turned. I hope he didn't notice us as he turned his head back slightly."

It made no difference, if he did, for, the curve passed, he was evidently feeding the gas faster than ever. We turned the curve also, the forward car something more than a quarter of a mile ahead of us.

"We must take a chance and close up on him," said Garrick, as he, too, accelerated his speed, not a difficult thing to do with the almost perfect racer of Warrington's. "He may turn off at a crossroad at any time, now."

Still our man kept on, bowling northward along the fine state road that led to one of the richest parts of the country.

He came to the attractive entrance to Tuxedo Park. Almost, I had expected him to turn in. At least I should not have been surprised if he had done so.

However, he kept on northward, past the entrance to the Park. We hung doggedly on.

Where was he going? I wondered whether Garrick might

have been wrong, after all. Half a mile lengthened into a mile. Still he was speeding on.

But Garrick had guessed right. Sure enough, at a cross road, the other car slowed down, then quickly swung around, off the main road.

"What are you going to do?" I asked Garrick quickly. "If we turn also, that will be too raw. Surely he'll notice that."

"Going to stop," cried Garrick, taking in the situation instantly. "Come on, Tom, jump out. We'll fake a little tire trouble, in case he should look around and see us stopping here. I'll keep the engine running."

We went back and stood ostentatiously by the rear wheel. Garrick bent over it, keeping his eye fixed on the other car, now perhaps half a mile along on the narrow crossroad.

It neared the top of a hill on the other side of the valley across which the road wound like a thin brown line, then dipped down over the crest and was lost on the other side.

Garrick leaped back into our car and I followed. He turned the bend almost on two wheels, and let her out as we swept down a short hill and then took the gentle incline on high speed, eating up the distance as though it had been inches instead of nearly a mile.

A short distance from the top of the hill, Garrick applied the brake, just in time so that the top of our car would not be visible to one who had passed on down the next incline into the valley beyond.

"Let us walk up the rest of the way," he said quickly, "and see what is on the other side of this hill."

We did so cautiously. Far down below us we could see the car which we had been trailing all the way up from the city, threading its way along the country road. We watched it, and as we did so, it slowed up and turned out, running up a sort of lane that led to what looked like a trim little country estate.

The car had stopped at an unpretentious house at the end of the lane. The driver got out and walked up to the back door, which seemed to be stealthily opened to admit him.

"Good!" exclaimed Garrick. "At last we are on a hot trail!"

CHAPTER XXI

THE SIEGE OF THE BANDITS

As we watched from the top of the hill, I wondered what Garrick's next move was to be. Surely he would not attempt to investigate the place yet. In fact, there seemed to be nothing that could be done now, as long as it was day-light, for any movement in this half-open country would have been viewed with suspicion by the occupants of the little house in the valley, whoever they might be.

We could not help viewing the place with a sort of awe. What secrets did the cottage hide, nestled down there in the valley among these green hills? Often I had heard that the gunmen of New York, when hard pressed, sought refuge in the country districts and mountains within a few miles of the city. There was something incongruous about it. Nature seemed so perfectly peaceful here that it was the very antithesis of those sections of the city in which he had found the gunman, whoever he was, indulging in practically every crime and vice of decadent civilization.

"So—the one they call the Boss has led up to the refuge of the Chief, the scientific gunman, at last," Garrick exclaimed, with marked satisfaction, as we turned and walked slowly back again to our car.

"Yes," I assented, "and now that we have found them—what are we to do with them?"

"It is still early in the day," Garrick remarked, looking at his watch. "They suspect no trouble up here. Here they evidently feel safe. No doubt they think we are still hunting for them fruitlessly in New York. I think we can afford to leave them here for a few hours. At any rate, I feel that I must return to the city. I must see Dillon, and then drop into my office, if we are to accomplish anything against them."

He had turned the car around and we made our way back to the main road, and then southward again, taking up in earnest the long return trip to the city and covering the distance in Warrington's racer in a much shorter time, now that we had not to follow another car and keep under cover. It was late in the afternoon, however, when we arrived and Garrick went directly to police headquarters where he held a hasty conference with Dillon.

Dillon was even more excited than we were when he learned how far we had gone in tracing out the scant clews that we had uncovered. As Garrick unfolded his plan, the commissioner immediately began to make arrangements to accompany us out into the country that night.

I did not hear all that was said, as Garrick and Dillon laid out their plans, but I could see that they were in perfect accord.

"Very well," I overheard Garrick, as we parted. "I shall go out in the car again. You will be up on the train?"

"Yes—on the seven-fifty," returned Dillon. "You needn't worry about my end of it. I'll be there with the goods—just the thing that you want. I have it."

"Fine," exclaimed Garrick, "I have to make a call at the office. I'll start as soon as I can, and try to beat you out."

They parted in good humour, for Dillon's passion for adventure was now thoroughly aroused and I doubt if we could have driven him off with a club, figuratively speaking.

At the office Garrick tarried only long enough to load the car with some paraphernalia which he had there, much of which, I knew, he had brought back with him after his study of police methods abroad. There were three coats of a peculiar texture, which he took from a wardrobe, a huge arrangement which looked like a reflector, a little thing that looked merely like the mouthpiece of a telephone transmitter, and a large heavy package which might have been anything from a field gun to a battering ram.

It was twilight when we arrived at the nearest railroad station to the little cottage in the valley, after another run up into the country in the car. Dillon who had come up by train to meet us, according to the arrangement with Garrick, was already waiting, and with him was one of the most trustworthy and experienced of the police department chauffeurs. Garrick looked about at the few loungers curiously, but there did not seem to be any of them who took any suspicious interest in new arrivals.

We four managed to crowd into a car built only for two, and Garrick started off. A few minutes later we arrived at the top of the hill from which we had already viewed the mysterious house earlier in the day. It was now quite dark. We had met no one since turning off into the crossroad, and could hear no sound except the continuous music of the night insects.

Just before crossing the brow of the last hill, we halted and Garrick turned out all the lights on the car. He was risking nothing that might lead to discovery yet. With the engine muffled down, we coasted slowly down the other side of the hill into the shadowy valley. There was no moon yet and we had to move cautiously, for there was only the faint light of the sky and stars to guide us.

What was the secret of that unpretentious little house below us? We peered out in the gathering blackness eagerly in the direction where we knew it must be, nestled among the trees. Whoever it sheltered was still there, and we could locate the place by a single gleam that came from an upper window. Whether there were lights below, we could not tell. If there were they must have been effectively concealed by blinds and shades.

"We'll stop here," announced Garrick at last when we had reached a point on the road a few hundred yards from the house.

He ran the car carefully off the road and into a little clearing in a clump of dark trees. We got out and pushed stealthily forward through the underbrush to the edge of the woods. There, on the slope, just a little way below us, stood the house of mystery.

Garrick and Dillon were busily conferring in an undertone, as I helped them bring the packages one after another from the car to the edge of the woods. Garrick had slipped the little telephone mouthpiece into his pocket, and was carrying the huge reflector carefully, so that it might not be injured in the darkness. I had the heavy coats of the peculiar texture over my arm, while Dillon and his man struggled along over the uncertain pathway, carrying between them the heavy, long, cylindrical package, which must have weighed some sixty pounds or so.

Garrick had selected as the site of our operations a corner of the grove where a very large tree raised itself as a landmark, silhouetted in black against a dark sky. We deposited the stuff there as he directed.

"Now, Jim," ordered Dillon, walking back to the car with his man, "I want you to take the car and go back along this road until you reach the top of the hill."

I could not hear the rest of the order, but it seemed that he was to meet someone who had preceded us on foot from the railway station and who must be about due to arrive. I did not know who or what it might be, but even the thought of someone else made me feel safer, for in so ticklish a piece of business as this, in dealing with at least a pair of desperate men such as we knew them to be in the ominously quiet little house, a second and even a third line of re-enforcements was not, I felt, amiss.

Garrick in the meantime had set to work putting into position the huge reflector. At first I thought it might be some method of throwing a powerful light on the house. But on closer examination I saw that it could not be a light. The reflector seemed to have been constructed so that in the focus was a peculiar coil of something, and to the ends of this coil, Garrick attached two wires which he fastened to an instrument, cylindrical, with a broadened end, like a telephone receiver.

Dillon, who had returned by this time, after sending his chauffeur back on his errand, appeared very much interested in what Garrick was doing.

"Now, Tom," said Garrick, "while I am fixing this thing, I wish you would help me by undoing that large package carefully."

While I was thus engaged, he continued talking with Dillon in a low voice, evidently explaining to him the use to which he wished the large reflector put.

I was working quickly to undo the large package, and as the wrappings finally came off, I could see that it was some bulky instrument that looked like a huge gun, or almost a mortar. It had a sort of barrel that might have been, say, forty inches in length, and where the breechlock should have been on an ordinary gun was a great hemispherical cavity. There was also a peculiar arrangement of springs and wheels in the butt.

"The coats?" he asked, as he took from the wrappings of the package several rather fragile looking tubes.

I had laid them down near us and handed them over to him. They were quite heavy, and had a rough feel.

"So-called bullet-proof cloth," explained Garrick. "At close range, quite powerful lunges of a dagger or knife recoil from it, and at a distance ordinary bullets rebound from it, flattened. We'll try it, anyway. It will do no harm, and it may do good. Now we are ready, Dillon."

"Wait just a minute," cautioned Dillon. "Let me see first whether that chauffeur has returned. He can run that engine so quietly that I myself can't hear it."

He had disappeared into the darkness toward the road, where he had despatched the car a few minutes before. Evidently the chauffeur had been successful in his mission, for Dillon was back directly with a hasty, "Yes, all right. He's backing the car around so that he can run it out on the road instantly in either direction. He'll be here in a moment."

Garrick had in the meantime been roughly sketching on the back of an old envelope taken from his pocket. Evidently he had been estimating the distance of the house from the tree back of which he stood, and worked with the light of a shaded pocket flashlight.

"Ready, then," he cried, jumping up and advancing to the peculiar instrument which I had unwrapped. He was in his element now. After all the weary hours of watching and preparation, here was action at last, and Garrick went to it like a starved man at food.

First he elevated the clumsy looking instrument pointed in the general direction of the house. He had fixed the angle at approximately that which he had hastily figured out on the envelope. Then he took a cylinder about twelve inches long, and almost half as much in diameter, a huge thing, constructed, it seemed, of a substance that was almost as brittle as an eggshell. Into the large hemispherical cavity in the breech of the gun he shoved it. He took another quick look at the light gleaming from the house in the darkness ahead of us.

"What is it?" I asked, indicating the "gun."

"This is what is known as the Mathiot gun," he explained as he brought it into action, "invented by a French scientist for the purpose, expressly, of giving the police a weapon to use against the automobile bandits who entrench themselves, when cornered, in houses and garages, as they have done in the outskirts of Paris, and as some anarchists did once in a house in London."

"What does it do?" asked Dillon, who had taken a great interest in the thing.

"It throws a bomb which emits suffocating gases without risking the lives of the police," answered Garrick. "In spite of the fragility of the bombs that I have here, it has been found that they will penetrate a wooden door or even a thin brick partition before the fuse explodes them. One bomb will render a room three hundred feet off uninhabitable in thirty seconds. Now—watch!"

He had exploded the gun by hand, striking the flat head of a hammer against the fulminating cap. The gun gave a bark. A low, whistling noise and a crash followed.

"Too short," muttered Garrick, elevating the angle of the gun a trifle.

Quite evidently someone was moving in the house. There was a shadow, as of someone passing between the light in the upper story and the window on our side of the house.

Again the gun barked, and another bomb went hurtling through the air. This time it hit the house squarely. Another followed in rapid succession, and the crash of glass told that it had struck a window. Garrick was sending them now as fast as he could. They had taken effect, too, for the light was out, whether extinguished by gases or by the hand of someone who realized that it afforded an excellent mark to shoot at. Still, it made no difference, now, for we had the range.

"The house must be full of the stifling gases," panted Garrick, as he stopped to wipe the perspiration from his face, after his rapid work, clad in the heavy coat. "No man could stand up against that. I wonder how our friend of the garage likes it, Tom? It is some of his own medicine—the Chief, I mean. He tried it on us on a small scale very successfully that night with his stupefying gun."

"I hope one of them hit him," ground out Dillon, who had no relish even for the recollection of that night. "What next? Do you have to wait until the gases clear away before we can make a break and go in there?"

Garrick had anticipated the question. Already he was buttoning up his long coat. We did the same, mechanically.

"No, Dillon. You and Jim stay here," ordered Garrick. "You will get the signal from us what to do next. Tom, come on."

He had already dashed ahead into the darkness, and I followed blindly, stumbling over a ploughed field, then a fence over which we climbed quickly, and found ourselves in the enclosure where was the house. I had no idea what we were running up against, but a dog which had been chained in the rear broke away from his fastening at sight of us, and ran at us with a lusty and savage growl. Garrick planted a shot squarely in his head.

Without wasting time on any formalities, such as ringing the bell, we kicked and battered in the back door. We paused a moment, not from fear but because the odor inside was terrific. No one could have stayed in that house and retained his senses. One by one, Garrick flung open the windows, and we were forced to stick our heads out every few minutes in order to keep our own breath.

From one room to another we proceeded, without finding anyone. Then we mounted to the second floor. The odour was worse there, but still we found no one.

The light on the third floor had been extinguished, as I have said. We made our way toward the corner where it had been. Room after room we entered, but still found no one. At last we came to a door that was locked. Together we wrenched it open.

Arthur B. Reeve

There was surely nothing for us to fear in this room, for a bomb had penetrated it, and had filled it completely. As we rushed in, Garrick saw a figure sprawled on the floor, near the bed, in the corner.

"Quick, Tom!" he shouted, "Open that other window. I'll attend to this man. He's groggy, anyhow."

Garrick had dropped down on his knees and had deftly slipped a pair of handcuffs on the unresisting wrists of the man. Then he staggered to my side at the open window, for air.

"Heavens—this is awful!" he gasped and sputtered. "I wonder where they all went?"

"Who is this fellow?" I asked.

"I don't know yet. I couldn't see."

A moment later, together, we had dragged the unconscious man to the window with us, while I fanned him with my hat and Garrick was wetting his face with water from a pitcher of ice on the table.

"Good Lord!" Garrick exclaimed suddenly, as in the fitful light he bent over the figure. "Do you see who it is?"

I bent down too and peered more closely.

It was Angus Forbes.

Strange to say, here was the young gambler whom we had seen at the gambling joint before it was raided, the long-lost and long-sought Forbes who had disappeared after the raid, and from whom no one had yet heard a word.

I did not know his story, but I knew enough to be sure that he had been in love with Violet himself, and, although Warrington had once come to his rescue and settled thousands of dollars of his gambling debts, was sore at Warrington for closing the gambling joint where he hoped ultimately to recoup his losses. More than that, he was probably equally sore at Warrington for winning the favour of the girl whose fortune might have settled his own debts, if he had had a free field to court her.

Why was Forbes here, I asked myself. The fumes of the bombs from the Mathiot gun may have got into my head but, at least as far as I could see, they had not made my mind any the less active. I felt that his presence here, apparently as one of the gang, explained many things.

Who, I reasoned, would have been more eager to "get" Warrington at any cost than he? I never had any love for the fellow, who had allowed his faults and his temptations so far to get the upper hand of him. I had felt a sort of pity at first, but the incident of the cancelled markers in the gambling joint and now the discovery of him here had changed that original feeling into one that was purely of disgust.

These thoughts were coursing through my fevered brain while Garrick was working hard to bring him around.

Suddenly a mocking voice came from the hall.

"Yes, it's Forbes, all right, and much good may it do you to have him!"

The door to the room, which opened outward, banged shut. The lock had been broken by us in forcing an entrance. There must have been two of them out in the hall, for we heard the noise and scraping of feet, as they piled up heavy

Arthur B. Reeve

furniture against the door, dragging it from the next room before we could do anything. Piece after piece was wedged in between our door and the opposite wall.

We could hear them taunt us as they worked, and I thought I recognised at once the voice of the stocky keeper of the garage, the Boss, whom I had heard so often before over our detectaphone. The other voice, which seemed to me to be disguised, I found somewhat familiar, yet I could not place it. It must have been, I thought, that of the man whom we had come to know and fear under the appellation of the Chief.

We could hear them laugh, now, as they cursed us and wished us luck with our capture. It was galling.

Evidently, too, they had not much use for Forbes, and, indeed, at such a crisis I do not think he would have been much more than an additional piece of animated impedimenta. Dissipation had not added anything to the physical prowess of Forbes.

With a parting volley of profanity, they stamped down the narrow stairs to the ground floor, and a few seconds afterward we could hear them back of the house, working over the machine which we had followed up from New York earlier in the day. Evidently there were several machines in the barn which served them as garage, but this was the handiest.

They had cranked it up, and were debating which way they should go.

"The shots came from the direction of the main road," the Boss said. "We had better go in the opposite direction. There may be more of them coming. Hurry up!"

At least, it seemed, there had been only three of them in this refuge which they had sought up in the hills and valleys of the Ramapos. Of that we could now be reasonably certain. One of them we had captured—and had ourselves been captured into the bargain.

I stuck my head out of the window to look at the other two down below, only to feel myself dragged unceremoniously back by Garrick.

"What's the use of taking that risk, Tom?" he expostulated. "One shot from them and you would be a dead one."

Fortunately they had not seen me, so intent were they on getting away. They had now seated themselves in the car and, as Garrick had suspected, could not resist delivering a parting shot at us, emptying the contents of an automatic blindly up at our window. Garrick and I were, as it. happened, busy on the opposite side of the room.

All thought of Forbes was dropped for the present. Garrick said not a word but continued at work in the corner of the room by the other broken window.

"Either they must have succeeded in getting out after the first shot and so escaped the fumes," muttered Garrick finally, "and hid in the stable, or, perhaps, they were out there at work anyhow. Still that makes little difference now. They must have seen us go in, have followed us quietly, and then caught us here."

With a hasty final imprecation, the car below started forward with a jerk and was swallowed up in the darkness.

CHAPTER XXII

THE MAN HUNT

Here we were, locked in a little room on the top floor of the mysterious house. I looked out of both windows. There was no way to climb down and it was too far to jump, especially in the uncertain darkness. I threw myself at the door. It had been effectually braced by our captors.

Garrick, in the meantime, had lighted the light again, and placed it by the window.

Forbes, now partly recovered, was rambling along, and Garrick, with one eye on him and the other on something which he was working over in the light, was too busy to pay much attention to my futile efforts to find a means of escape.

At first we could not make out what it was that Forbes was trying to tell us, but soon, as the fresh air in the room revived him, his voice became stronger. Apparently he recognised us and was trying to offer an explanation of his presence here.

"He kidnapped me—brought me here," Forbes was muttering. "Three days—I've been shut up in this room."

"Who brought you here?" I demanded sharply.

"I don't know his name—man at the gambling place—after the raid - said he'd take me in his car somewhere—from the other place back of it—last I remember—must have drugged me—woke up here—all I know."

"You've been a prisoner, then?" I queried.

"Yes," he murmured.

"A likely story," I remarked, looking questioningly at Garrick who had been listening but had not ceased his own work, whatever it was. "What are you going to do, Guy? We can't stay here and waste time over such talk as this while they are escaping. They must be almost to the road now, and turning down in the opposite direction from Dillon and his man."

Garrick said nothing. Either he was too busy solving our present troubles or he was, like myself, not impressed by Forbes' incoherent story. He continued to adjust the little instrument which I had seen him draw from his pocket and now recognised as the thing which looked like a telephone transmitter. Only, the back of it seemed to gleam with a curious brightness under the rays of the light, as he handled it.

"They have somehow contrived to escape the effect of the bombs," he was saying, "and have surprised us in the room on the top floor where the light is. We are up here with a young fellow named Forbes, whom we have captured. He's the young man that I saw several times at the gambling joint and was at dinner with Warrington the night when the car was stolen. He was pretty badly overcome by the fumes, but I've brought him around. He either doesn't know much or won't tell what he knows. That doesn't make any difference now, though. They have escaped in a car. They are leaving by the road. Wait. I'll see whether they have reached it yet.

No, it's too dark to see and they have no light on the car. But they must have turned. They said they were going in the direction opposite from you."

"Well?" I asked, mystified. "What of it? I know all that, already."

"But Dillon doesn't," replied Garrick, in great excitement now. "I knew that we should have to have some way of communicating with him instantly if this fellow proved to be as resourceful as I believed him to be. So I thought of the radiophone or photophone of Dr. Alexander Graham Bell. I have really been telephoning on a beam of light."

"Telephoning on a beam of light?" I repeated incredulously.

"Yes," he explained, feeling now at liberty to talk since he had delivered his call for help. "You see, I talk into this transmitter. The simplest transmitter for this purpose is a plane mirror of flexible material, silvered mica or microscope glass. Against the back of this mirror my voice is directed. In the carbon transmitter of the telephone a variable electrical resistance is produced by the pressure on the diaphragm, based on the fact that carbon is not as good a conductor of electricity under pressure as when not. Here, the mouthpiece is just a shell supporting a thin metal diaphragm to which the mirror on the back is attached, an apparatus for transforming the air vibrations produced by the voice into light vibrations of the projected beam, which is reflected from this light here in the room. The light reflected is thus thrown into vibrations corresponding to those in the diaphragm."

"And then?" I asked impatiently.

"That varying beam of light shoots out of this room, and is

caught by the huge reflector which you saw me set up at the foot of that tall tree which you can just see against the dark sky over there. That parabolic mirror gathers in the scattered rays, focusses them on the selenium cell which you saw in the middle of the reflector, and that causes the cell to vary the amount of electric current passing through it from a battery of storage cells. It is connected with a very good telephone receiver. Every change in the beam of light due to the vibrations of my voice is caught by that receiving mirror, and the result is that the diaphragm in the receiver over there which Dillon is holding to his ear responds. The thing is good over several hundred yards, perhaps miles, sometimes. Only, I wish it would work both ways. I would like to feel sure that Dillon gets me."

I looked at the simple little instrument with a sort of reverence, for on it depended the momentous question of whether we should be released in time to pursue the two who were escaping in the automobile.

"You'll have to hurry," continued Garrick, speaking into his transmitter. "Give the signal. Get the car ready. Anything, so long as it is action. Use your own judgment."

There he was, flashing a message out of our prison by an invisible ray that shot across the Cimmerian darkness to the point where we knew that our friends were waiting anxiously. I could scarcely believe it. But Garrick had the utmost faith in the ability of the radiophone to make good.

"They MUST have started by this time," he cried, craning his neck out of the window and looking in every direction.

Forbes was still rambling along, but Garrick was not paying any attention to him. Instead, he began rummaging the room for possible evidence, more for something to do than because he hoped to find anything, while we were waiting anxiously for something to happen.

An exclamation from Garrick, however, brought me to his side. Tucked away in a bureau drawer under some soiled linen that plainly belonged to Forbes, he drew out what looked like a single blue-steel tube about three inches long. At its base was a hard-rubber cap, which fitted snugly into the palm of the hand as he held it. His first and middle fingers encircled the barrel, over a steel ring. A pull downward and the thing gave a click.

"Good that it wasn't loaded," Garrick remarked. "I knew what the thing was, all right, but I didn't think the spring was as delicate as all that. It is a new and terrible weapon of destruction of human life, one that can be carried by the thug or the burglar and no one be the wiser, unless he has occasion to use it. It is a gun that can be concealed in the palm of the hand. A pull downward on that spring discharges a thirty-two calibre, centre fire cartridge. The most dangerous feature of it is that the gun can be carried in an upper vest pocket as a fountain pen, or in a trousers pocket as a penknife."

I looked with added suspicion now, if not a sort of respect, on the young man who was tossing, half conscious, on the bed. Was he, after all, not the simple, gullible Forbes, but a real secret master of crime?

Garrick, keen though he had been over the discovery, was in reality much more interested just now in the result of his radiophone message. What would be the outcome?

I had been startled to see that almost instantly after his second call over the radiophone there seemed to rise on all sides of us lights and the low baying of dogs.

"What's all that?" I asked Garrick.

"Dillon had a dozen or so police dogs shipped up here quietly," answered Garrick, now straining his eyes and ears eagerly. "He started them out each in charge of an officer as soon as they arrived. I hope they had time to get around in that other direction and close in. That was what he sent the chauffeur back to see about, to make sure that they were placed by the man who is the trainer of the pack."

"What kind of dogs are they?"

"Some Airedales, but mostly Belgian sheep dogs. There is one in the pack, Cherry, who has a wonderful reputation. A great deal depends, now, on our dog-detectives."

"But," I objected, "what good will they be? Our men are in an automobile."

"We thought of that," replied Garrick confidently. "Here they are, at last," he cried, as a car swung up the lane from the road and stopped with a rush under our window. He leaned out and shouted, "Dillon—up here—quick!"

It was Dillon and his chauffeur, Jim. A moment later there was a tremendous shifting and pulling of heavy pieces of furniture in the hall, and, as the door swung open, the honest face of the commissioner appeared, inquiring anxiously if we were all right.

"Yes, all right," assured Garrick. "Come on, now. There isn't a minute to lose. Send Jim up here to take charge of Forbes. I'll drive the car myself."

Garrick accomplished in seconds what it takes minutes to tell. The chauffeur had already turned the car around and it was ready to start. We jumped in, leaving him to go upstairs and keep the manacled Forbes safely.

We gained the road and sped along, our lights now lighted and showing us plainly what was ahead. The dust-laden air told us that we were right as we turned into the narrow crossroad. I wondered how we were ever going to overtake them after they had such a start, at night, too, over roads which were presumably familiar to them.

"Drive carefully," shouted Dillon soon, "it must be along here, somewhere, Garrick."

A moment before we had been almost literally eating the dust the car ahead had raised. Garrick slowed down as we approached a bend in the road.

There, almost directly in our path, stood a car, turned half across the road and jammed up into a fence. I could scarcely believe it. It was the bandit's car—deserted!

"Good!" exclaimed Dillon as Garrick brought our own car to a stop with a jerk only a few feet away.

I looked about in amazement, first at the empty car and then into the darkness on either side of the road. For the moment I could not explain it. Why had they abandoned the car, especially when they had every prospect of eluding us in it?

They had not been forced to turn out for anybody, for no other vehicle had passed us. Was it tire trouble or engine trouble? I turned to the others for an explanation.

"I thought it must be about here," cried Dillon. "We had one of my men place an obstruction in the road. They didn't run into it, which shows clever driving, but they had to turn so sharply that they ran into the fence. I guess they realised that there was no use in turning and trying to go back."

"They have taken to the open country," shouted Garrick, leaping up on the seat of our car and looking about in a vain endeavour to catch some sign of them.

All was still, save here and there the sharp, distant bark of a dog.

"I wonder which way they went?" he asked, looking down at us.

CHAPTER XXIII

THE POLICE DOG

Dillon pulled a whistle from his pocket and blew a short blast sharply. Far down the road, we could hear faintly an answering bark. It came nearer.

"They're taught to obey a police whistle and nothing else," remarked Dillon, with satisfaction. "I wonder which one of the dogs that was. By the way, just keep out of sight as much as you can—get back up in our car. They are trained to worry anyone who hasn't a uniform. I'll take this dog in charge. I hope it's Cherry. She ought to be around here, if the men obeyed my orders. The others aren't keen on a scent even when it is fresh, but Cherry is a dandy and I had the man bring her up purposely."

We got back into our car and waited impatiently. Across the hills now and then we could catch the sounds of dogs scouting around here and there. It seemed as if every dog in the valley had been aroused. On the other slope of the hill from the main road we could see lights in the scattered houses.

"I doubt whether they have gone that way," commented Garrick following my gaze. "It looks less settled over here to the right of the road, in the direction of New York."

The low baying of the dog which had answered Dillon's call was growing nearer every moment. At last we could hear it quite close, at the deserted car ahead.

Cherry seemed to have many of the characteristics of the wild, prehistoric animal, among them the full, upright ears of the wild dog, which are such a great help to it. She was a fine, alert, up-standing dog, hardy, fierce, and literally untiring, of a tawny light brown like a lioness, about the same size and somewhat of the type of the smooth-coated collie, broad of chest and with a full brush of tail.

Untamed though she seemed, she was perfectly under Dillon's control, and rendered him absolute and unreasoning obedience.

"Now, Cherry, nice dog," we heard Dillon encouraging, "Here, up here. And here."

He was giving the dog the scent from the deserted car. His voice rang out sharply in the night air, "Come on Garrick and Marshall. She's got it. I've got her on leash. Follow along, now, just a few feet behind."

Cherry was on the trail and it was a hot one. We could just see her magnificent head, narrow and dome-like, between the keen ears. She was working like a regular sleuthhound, now, too, slowly, picking up the trail and following it, baying as she went.

She was now going without a halt or falter. Nose to the ground, she had leaped from the bandit's car and made straight across a field in the direction that Garrick had suspected they would take, only a little to the west.

"This is a regular, old-fashioned man hunt," called back Dillon, as we followed the dog and himself, as best we could.

It was pitch dark, but we plunged ahead over fields and through little clumps of trees, around hedges, and over fences.

There was no stopping, no cessation of the deep baying of the dog. Cherry was one of the best and most versatile that the police had ever acquired and trained.

We came to the next crossroad, and the dog started up in the direction of the main road, questing carefully.

We had gone not a hundred feet when a dark object darted out of the bushes at the side of the road, and I felt myself unceremoniously tumbled off my feet.

Garrick leaped aside, with a laugh.

"Dillon," he shouted ahead at the top of his voice, "one of the Airedales has discovered Marshall. Come back here. Lie still, Tom. The dog is trained to run between the legs and trip up anyone without a police uniform. By Jupiter—here's another one—after me. Dillon—I say—Dillon!"

The commissioner came back, laughing at our plight, and called off the dogs, who were now barking furiously. We let him get a little ahead, calling the Airedales to follow him. They were not much good on the scent, but keen and intelligent along the lines of their training, and perfectly willing to follow Dillon, who was trusting to the keen sense of Cherry.

A little further down, the fugitives had evidently left the road after getting their bearings.

"They must have heard the dogs," commented Garrick. "They are doubling on their tracks, now, and making for the Ramapo River in the hope of throwing the dogs off the scent. That's the game. It's an old trick."

We came, sure enough, in a few minutes to the river. That had indeed been their objective point. Cherry was baffled. We stuck close to Dillon, after our previous experience, as we stopped to talk over hastily what to do.

Had they gone up or down, or had they crossed? There was not much time that we could afford to lose here in speculation if we were going to catch them.

Cherry was casting backward in an instinctive endeavour to pick up the trail. Dillon had taken her across and she had not succeeded in finding the scent on the opposite bank for several hundred yards on either side.

"They started off toward the southwest," reasoned Garrick quickly. "Then they turned in this direction. The railroads are over there. Yes, that is what they would make for. Dillon," he called, "let us follow the right bank of the river down this way, and see if we can't pick them up again."

The river was shallow at this point, but full of rocks, which made it extremely hard, if not dangerous, to walk even close to the bank in the darkness. "I don't think they'd stand for much of this sort of going," remarked Garrick. "A little of it would satisfy them, and they'd strike out again."

He was right. Perhaps five minutes later, after wading in the cold water, clinging as close to the bank as we could, we came to a sort of rapids. Cherry, who had been urged on by

Dillon, gave a jerk at her leash, as she sniffed along the bank.

"She has it," cried Garrick, springing up the bank after Dillon.

I followed and we three men and three dogs struck out again in earnest across country.

We had come upon a long stretch of woods, and the brambles and thick growth made the going exceedingly difficult. Still, if it was hard for us now, it must have been equally hard for them as they broke through in the first place.

At last we came to the end of the woods. The trail was now fresher than ever, and Dillon had difficulty in holding Cherry back so that the rest of us could follow. As we emerged from the shadow of the trees into the open field, it seemed as if guns were blazing on all sides of us.

We were almost up with them. They had separated and were not half a mile away, firing at random in our direction, as they heard the dogs. Dillon drew up, Cherry tugging ahead. He turned to the Airedales. They had already taken in the situation, and were now darting ahead at what they could see, if not scent.

I felt a "ping!" on my chest. I scarcely realized what it was until I heard something drop the next instant in the stubble at my feet, and felt a smarting sensation as if a sharp blow had struck me. I bent down and from the stubble picked up a distorted bullet.

"These bullet-proof coats are some good, anyhow, at a distance," remarked Garrick, close beside me, as he took the bullet from my fingers. "Duck! Back among the trees—until we get our bearings!"

Another bullet had whizzed just past his arm as he spoke.

We dodged back among the trees, and slowly skirted the edge of the wood, where it bent around a little on the flank of the position from which the continuous firing was coming.

At the edge we stopped again. We could go no further without coming out into the open, and the moon, just rising, above the trees, made us an excellent mark under such conditions. Garrick peered out to determine from just where they were firing.

"Lucky for us that we had these coats," he muttered, "or they would have croaked us, before we knew it. These are our old friends, the anaesthetic bullets, too. Even a little scratch from one of them and we should be hors de combat for an hour or two."

"Shall we take a chance?" urged Dillon.

"Just a minute," cautioned Garrick, listening.

The barking of the Airedales had ceased suddenly. Cherry was straining at her leash to go.

"They have winged the two dogs," exclaimed Garrick. "Yes—we must try it now—at any cost."

We broke from the cover, taking a chance, separating as much as we could, and pushing ahead rapidly, Dillon under his breath keeping Cherry from baying as much as possible.

I had expected a sharp fusillade to greet us as we advanced and wondered whether the coats would stand it at closer range. Instead, the firing seemed to have ceased altogether.

A quick dash and we had crossed the stretch of open field that separated us from a dark object which now loomed up, and from behind which it seemed had come the firing. As we approached, I saw it was a shed beside the railroad, which was depressed at this point some twelve or fifteen feet.

"They kept us off just long enough," exclaimed Garrick, glancing up at the lights of the block signals down the road. "They must be desperate, all right. Why, they must have jumped a freight as it slowed down for the curve, or perhaps one of them flagged it and held it up. See? The red signal shows that a train has just gone through toward New York. There is no chance to wire ahead, either, from this Ducktown siding. Here's where they stood—look!"

Garrick had picked up a handful of exploded cartridge shells, while he was speaking. They told a mute story of the last desperate stand of the gunmen.

"I'll keep these," he said, shoving them into his pocket. "They may be of some use later on in connecting to-night's doings with what has gone before."

We looked at each other blankly. There was nothing more to do that night but to return to the now deserted house in the valley where we had left Forbes in charge of Dillon's man.

Toilsomely and disgusted, we trudged back in silence.

Garrick, however, refused to be discouraged. Late as it was, he insisted on making a thorough search of the captured house. It proved to be a veritable arsenal. Here it seemed that all the new and deadly weapons of the scientific gunman had been made. The barn, turned into half garage and half workshop, was a mine of interest.

We found it unlocked and entered, Garrick flashing a light about.

"There's a sight that would do McBirney's eyes good," he exclaimed as he bent the rays of the light before us.

Before us, in the back of the barn, stood Warrington's stolen car - at last.

"They won't plot anything more—at least not up here," remarked Garrick, bending over it.

In the house, we found Jim still with Forbes, who was now completely recovered. In the possession of his senses, Forbes' tongue which the anaesthetic gases seemed to have loosened, now became suddenly silent again. But he stuck doggedly to his story of kidnapping, although he would not or could not add anything to it. Who the kidnapper was he swore he did not know, except that he had known his face well, by sight, at the gambling joint.

I could make nothing of Forbes. But of one thing I was sure. Even if we had not captured the scientific gunman, we had dealt him a severe and crushing blow. Like Garrick, I had begun to look upon the escape philosophically.

CHAPTER XXIV

THE FRAME-UP

Although I felt discouraged on our return to the city, the morning following our exciting adventure at the mysterious house in the Ramapo valley, Garrick, who never let anything ruffle him long, seemed quite cheerful.

"Cheer up, Tom," he encouraged. "We are on the home stretch now."

"Perhaps—if they don't beat us to the tape," I answered disconsolately. "What are you going to do next?"

"While you were snatching a little sleep, I was rummaging around and found a number of letters in a table drawer, up there. One was a note, evidently to the garage keeper, and signed merely, 'Chief.' I'll wager that the handwriting is the same as that in the blackmailing letter to Miss Winslow."

"What of it?" I asked, refusing to be comforted. "We haven't got him and the prospects—"

"No, we haven't got him," interrupted Garrick, "but the note was just a line to tell the Boss, who seemed to have been up there in the country at the time, to meet the Chief at 'the

Joint,' on Second Avenue."

I nodded, but before I could speak, he added, "It didn't say any more, but I think I know the place. It is the old International Cafe, a regular hang-out for crooks, where they come to gamble away the proceeds of their crimes in stuss, the great game of the East Side, now. Anyhow, we'll just drop into the place. We may not find them, but we'll have an interesting time. Then, there is the possibility of getting a strangle hold on someone, anyhow."

Garrick was evidently figuring on having driven our gunman back into the haunts of the underworld.

There seemed to be no other course that presented itself and therefore, rather than remain inactive until something new turned up, I consented to accompany him in his excursion.

Forbes, still uncommunicatively protesting that he would say nothing until he had an opportunity to consult a lawyer, had been taken down to New York by Dillon during the morning and was lodged in a West Side prison under a technical charge which was sufficient to hold him until Garrick could investigate his case and fix his real status.

We had taken a cross-town car, with the intention of looking over the dive where Garrick believed the crooks might drop in. The ride itself was uninteresting, but not so by any means the objective point of our journey.

Over on the East Side, we found the International Cafe, and slouched into the back room. It was not the room devoted to stuss, but the entrance to it, which Garrick informed me was through a heavy door concealed in a little hallway, so that its very existence would not be suspected except by the initiate.

We made no immediate attempt to get into the hang-out proper, which was a room perhaps thirty feet wide and seventy feet deep. Instead, we sat down at one of the dirty, round tables, and ordered something from the waiter, a fat and oily Muscowitz in a greasy and worn dinner coat.

It seemed that in the room where we were had gathered nearly every variety of the populous underworld. I studied the men and women at the tables curiously, without seeming to do so. But there could be no concealment here. Whatever we might be, they seemed to know that we were not of them, and they greeted us with black looks and now and then a furtive scowl.

It was not long, however, before it became evident that in some way word had been passed that we were not mere sightseers. Perhaps it was by a sort of wireless electric tension that seemed to pervade the air. At any rate, it was noticeable.

"There's no use staying here," remarked Garrick to me under his breath, affecting not to notice the scowls, "unless we do something. Are you game for trying to get into the stuss joint?"

He said it with such determination to go himself that I did not refuse. I had made up my mind that the only thing to do was to follow him, wherever he went.

Garrick rose, stretched himself, yawned as though bored, and together we lounged out into the public hall, just as someone from the outside clamoured for admission to the stuss joint through the strong door.

The door had already been opened, when Garrick deftly inserted his shoulder. Through the crack in the door, I could see the startled roomful of players of all degrees in crookdom, in the thick, curling tobacco smoke.

The man at the door called out to Garrick to get out, and raised his arm to strike. Garrick caught his fist, and slowly with his powerful grip bent it back until the man actually writhed. As his wrist went back by fractions of an inch, his fingers were forced to relax. I knew the trick. It was the scientific way to open a clenched fist. As the tendons refused to stretch any farther, his fingers straightened, and a murderous looking blackjack clattered to the floor.

All was confusion. Money which was on the various tables disappeared as if by magic. Cards were whisked away as if a ghost had taken them. In a moment there was no more evidence of gambling than is afforded by any roomful of men, so easy was it to hide the paraphernalia, or, rather, lack of paraphernalia of stuss.

It was the custom, I knew, for criminals, after they had made a haul to retire into such places as these stuss parlors, not only to spend the proceeds of their robberies, but for protection. Even though they were unmercifully fleeced by the gamblers, they might depend on them to warn of the approach of the "bulls" and if possible count on being hidden or spirited off to safety.

Apparently we had come just at a time when there were some criminals in hiding among the players. It was the only explanation I could offer of the strange action that greeted our simple attempt to gain admission to the stuss room. Whether they were criminals who had really made a haul or mere fugitives from justice, I could not guess. But that a warning had been given the man at the door to be on his guard, seemed evident from the manner in which we had been met.

Arthur B. Reeve

There was a rush of feet in the room. I expected that we would be overwhelmed. Instead, as together we pushed on the now half-open door, the room emptied like a sieve. Whoever it might be who had taken refuge there had probably disappeared, among the first, by tacit understanding of the rest, for the whole thing had the air of being run off according to instructions.

"It's a collar!" had sounded through the room, the moment we had appeared at the door, and it was now empty.

I wondered whether the letter which Garrick had found might not, after all, have brought us straight to the last resort of those whom we sought.

"Where have they gone?" I panted, as the door opened at last, and we found only one man in the place.

There he stood apparently ready to be arrested, in fact courting it if we could show the proper authority, since he knew that it would be only a question of hours when he would be out again and the game would be resumed, in full blast.

The man shook his head blankly in answer to my question.

"There must be a trap door somewhere," cried Garrick. "It is no use to find it. They are all on the street by this time. Quick—before anyone catches us in the rear."

We had been not a moment too soon in gaining the street. Though we had done nothing but attempt to get into the stuss room, ostensibly as players, the crowd in the cafe was pressing forward.

On the street, we saw men filing quickly from a cellar, a few doors down the block. We mingled with the excited crowd in order to cover ourselves.

"That must have been where the trap door and passage led," whispered Garrick.

A familiar figure ducked out of the cellar, surrounded by others, and the crowd made for two taxicabs standing on the opposite side of the street near a restaurant which was really not a tough joint but made a play at catering to people from uptown who wanted a taste of near-crime and did not know when they were being buncoed.

Another cab swung up to the stand, just as the first two pulled away. Its sign was up: "Vacant."

Quick as a flash, Garrick was in it, dragging me after him. The driver must have thought that we, too, were escaping, for he needed only one order from Garrick to leap ahead in the wake of the cabs which had already started.

A moment later, Garrick's head was out of the window. He had drawn his revolver and was pegging away at the tires of the cabs ahead. An answering shot came back to us. Meanwhile, a policeman at a corner leaped on a passing trolley and urged the motorman to put on the full power in a vain effort to pursue us as we swept by up the broad avenue.

Even the East Side, accustomed to frequent running fights on the streets between rival gunmen and gangs, was roused by such an outburst. The crack of revolver shots, the honking of horns, the clang of the trolley bell, and the shouts of men along the street brought hundreds to the windows, as the cars lurched and swayed up the avenue.

The cars ahead swerved to dodge a knot of pedestrians, but

their pace never slackened. Then the rearmost of the two began to buck and almost leap off the roadway. There came a rattle and roar from the rear wheels which told that the tires had been punctured and that the heavy wheels were riding on their rims, cutting the deflated tubes. At a cross street the first car turned, just in time to avoid a truck, and dodged down a maze of side streets, but the second ran squarely into the truck.

As the first car disappeared we caught a glimpse of a man leaning out of it. He seemed to be swinging something around and around at arm's length. Suddenly he let it go and it shot high up in the air on the roof of a tenement house.

"The automobile is the most dangerous weapon ever used by criminals," muttered Garrick, as the first car shot down through a mass of trucking which had backed up and shifted, making pursuit momentarily more impossible for us. "These people know how to use the automobile, too. But we've got someone here, anyhow," he cried, leaping out and pushing aside the crowd that had collected about the wrecked car.

In the bottom of it we found a man, stunned and crumpled into a heap. Blood flowed from his arm where one of the bullets had struck him. Several bullets had struck the back of the cab and both tires were cut by them.

As I came up and looked over Garrick's shoulder at the prostrate and unconscious figure in the car, I could not restrain an exclamation of surprise.

It was the garage keeper, the Boss—at last!

Policemen had come up in the meantime, and several minutes were consumed while Garrick proved to them his identity.

"What was that thing the fellow in the forward car whirled over his head?" I whispered.

"A revolver, I think," returned Garrick. "That's a favourite trick of the gunmen. With a stout cord tied to a gun you can catapult it far enough to destroy the evidence that will hold you under the Sullivan law, at least. I mean to get that gun as soon as we are through with this fellow here."

Someone had turned in a call for an ambulance which came jangling up soon after, and we stood in a group close to the young surgeon as he worked to bring around the captured gangster.

"Where's the Chief?" he mumbled, dazed.

Garrick motioned to us to be quiet.

The man rambled on with a few inconsequential remarks, then opened his eyes, caught sight of the white coated surgeon working over him, of us standing behind, and of the crowd about him.

Memory of what had happened flitted back to him. With an effort he was himself again, close-mouthed, after the manner of the gangsters.

The surgeon had done all in his power and the man was sufficiently recovered to be taken to the hospital, now, under arrest. As far as we were concerned, our work was done. The Boss could be found now, at any time that we needed him, but that he would speak all the traditions of gangland made impossible.

I wondered what Garrick would do. As for myself, I had no idea what move to make.

Arthur B. Reeve

It surprised me, therefore, to see him with a smile of satisfaction on his face.

"I'll see you this afternoon, Tom," he said merely, as the ambulance bore the wounded Boss away. "Meanwhile, I wish you'd take the time to go over to headquarters and give Dillon our version of this affair. Tell him to hold to-night open, too. I have a little work to do this afternoon, and I'll call him up later."

Dillon, I found, was overjoyed when I reported to him the capture of at least one man whom we had failed to get the night before.

"Things seem to be clearing up, after all," he remarked. "Tell Garrick I shall hold open to-night for him. Meanwhile, good luck, and let me know the moment you get any word about the Chief. He must have been in. that first cab, all right."

As I left Dillon's office, I ran into Herman in the hall, coming in. I bowed to him and he nodded surlily. Evidently, I thought, he had heard of the result of our activities. I did not ask him what progress he had made in the case, for I had had experience with professional jealousy before, and thought that the less said on the subject the better.

Recalling what Garrick had said, I curbed my impatience as best I could, in order to give him ample time to complete the work that he had to do. It was not until the middle of the afternoon that I rejoined him in his office.

I found him at work at a table, still, with a microscope and an arrangement which I recognised as the apparatus for making microphotographs. Several cartridges, carefully labelled, were lying before him, as well as the peculiar pistol we had found when we had captured Forbes in the little room. There were also the guns we had captured in the garage and one found in the cab which we had chased and wrecked.

On the end of the table was a large number of photographs of a most peculiar nature. I picked up one. It looked like an enlarged photograph of an orange, or like some of the pictures which the astronomers make of the nearer planets.

"What are these?" I asked curiously, as he leaned back from his work, with a smile of quiet satisfaction.

"That is a collection of microphotographs which I have gathered," he answered, adding, "as well as some that I have just made. I hope to use them in a little stereopticon entertainment I am arranging to-night for those who have been interested in the case."

Garrick smiled. "Have you ever heard?" he asked, "that the rounded end of the firing pin of every rifle when it is examined under a microscope bears certain irregularities of marking different from those of every other firing pin and that the primer of every shell fired in a rifle is impressed with the particular markings of that firing pin?"

I had not, but Garrick went on, "I know that it is true. Such markings are distinctive for each rifle and can be made by no other. I have taken rifles bearing numbers preceding and following that of a particular one, as well as a large number of other firing pins. I have tried the rifles and the firing pins, one by one, and after I made microphotographs of the firing pins with special reference to the rounded ends and also photographs of the corresponding rounded depressions in the primers fired by them, it was forced upon me that cartridges fired by each individual firing pin could be positively identified."

I had been studying the photographs. It was a new idea, and it appealed to me strongly. "How about revolvers?" I asked quickly.

"Well, Dr. Balthazard, the French criminologist, has made experiments on the identification of revolver bullets and has a system that might be compared to that of Bertillon for identifying human beings. He has showed by greatly enlarged photographs that every gun barrel leaves marks on a bullet and that the marks are always the same for the same barrel but never identical for two different barrels. He has shown that the hammer of a revolver, say a centre fire, strikes the cartridge at a point which is never the exact centre of the cartridge, but is always the same for the same weapon. He has made negatives of bullets nearly a foot wide. Every detail appears very distinctly and it can be decided with absolute certainty whether a certain bullet or cartridge was fired by a certain revolver."

He had picked up one of the microphotographs and was looking at it attentively through a small glass.

"You will see," he explained, "on the edge of this photograph a rough sketch calling attention to a mark like an L which is the chief characteristic of this hammer, although there are other detailed markings which show well under the microscope but not in a photograph. You will note that the marks on a hammer are reversed on the primer in the same way that a metal type and the character printed by it are reversed as regards one another. Moreover, depressions on the end of a hammer become raised on the primer and raised markings on the hammer become depressions on the primer.

"Now, here is another. You can see that it is radically different from the first, which was from the cartridge used in killing poor Rena Taylor. This second one is from that gun which I found on the tenement roof this morning. It lacks the L mark as well as the concentric circles. Here is another. Its chief characteristics are a series of pits and elevations which, examined under the microscope and measured, will be found to afford a set of characters utterly different from those of any other hammer.

"In short," he concluded with an air of triumph, "the ends of firing pins are turned and finished in a lathe by the use of tools designed for that purpose. The metal tears and works unevenly so that microscopical examination shows many pits, lines, circles, and irregularities. The laws of chance are as much against two of these firing pins or hammers having the same appearance under the microscope as they are against the thumb prints of two human subjects being identical."

I picked up the curious little arrangement which we had found in the drawer in Forbes' room and examined it closely.

"I have been practicing with that pistol, if you may call it that," he remarked, "on cartridges of my own and examining the marks made by the peculiar hammer. I have studied marks of the gun which we found on the roof. I have compared them with the marks on cartridges which we have picked up at the finding of Rena Taylor's body, at the garage that night of the stupefying bullet, with bullets such as were aimed at Warrington, with others, both cartridges and bullets, at various times, and the conclusion is unescapable."

Who, I asked myself, was the scientific gunman? I knew it was useless to try to hurry Garrick. First, by a sort of intuition he had picked him out, then by the evidence of hammer and bullet he had made it practically certain. But I knew that to his scientific mind nothing but absolute certainty would suffice.

While I was waiting for him to proceed, he had already begun to work on some apparatus behind a screen at the end of his office. Close to the wall at the left was a stereopticon which, as nearly as I could make out, shot a beam of light through a tube to a galvanometer about three feet distant. In front of this beam whirled a five-spindled wheel governed by a chronometer which was so accurate, he said, that it erred only a second a day.

Between the poles of the galvanometer was stretched a slender thread of fused quartz plated with silver. It was the finest thread I could imagine, only a thousandth of a millimeter in diameter, far too tenuous to be seen. Three feet further away was a camera with a moving plate holder which carried a sensitized photographic plate. Its movement was regulated by a big fly-wheel at the extreme right.

"You see," remarked Garrick, now engrossed on the apparatus and forgetting the hammer evidence for the time, "the beam of light focussed on that fine thread in the galvanometer passes to this photographic plate. It is intercepted by the five spindles of the wheel, which turns once a second, thus marking the picture off in exact fifths of a second. The vibrations of the thread are enormously magnified on the plate by a lens and produce a series of wavy or zigzag lines. I have shielded the sensitized plate by a wooden hood which permits no light to strike it except the slender ray that is doing the work. The plate moves across the field slowly, its speed regulated by the fly-wheel. Don't you think it is neat and delicate? All these movements are produced by one of the finest little electric motors I ever saw."

I could not get the idea of the revolvers out of my head so quickly. I agreed with him, but all I could find to say was, "Do you think there was more than this one whom they call the Chief engaged in the shootings?"

"I can't say absolutely anything more than I have told you, yet," he answered in a tone that seemed to discourage further questioning along that line.

He continued to work on the delicate apparatus with its thread stretched between the stationary magnets of the galvanometer, a thread so delicate that it might have been spun by a microscopic spider, so light that no scales made by human hands could weigh it, so slender that the mind could hardly grasp it. It was about one-third the diameter of a red corpuscle of blood and its weight had been estimated as about .00685 milligrams, truly a fairy thread. It was finer than the most delicate cobweb and could be seen with the naked eye only when a strong light was thrown on it so as to catch the reflection.

"All I can say is," he admitted, "that the bullets which committed this horrible series of crimes have been proven all to be shot from the same gun, presumably, I think I shall show, by the same hand, and that hand is the same that wrote the blackmailing letter."

"Whose gun was it?" I asked. "Was there a way to connect it and the bullets and the cartridges with the owner—four things, all separated—and then that owner with the curious and tragic succession of events that had marked the case since the theft of Warrington's car?"

Garrick had apparently completed his present work of adjusting the delicate apparatus. He was now engaged on another piece which also had a powerful light in it and an attachment which bore a strong resemblance to a horn.

He paused a moment, regarding me quizzically. "I think you'll find it sufficiently novel to warrant your coming, Tom," he added. "I have already invited Dillon and his man, Herman, over the telephone just before you came in. McBirney will be there, and Forbes, of course. He'll have to come, if I want him. By the way, I wish you'd get in touch with Warrington and see how he is. If it is all right, tell him that I'd like to have him escort Miss Winslow and her aunt here, to-night. Meanwhile I shall find out how our friend the Boss is getting on. He ought to be here, at any cost, and I've put it off until to-night to make sure that he'll be in fit condition to come. To-night at nine— here in this office—remember," he concluded gayly. "In the meantime, not a word to anybody about what you have seen here this afternoon."

CHAPTER XXV

THE SCIENTIFIC GUNMAN

Our little audience arrived one by one, and, as master of ceremonies, it fell to me to greet them and place them as much at ease as the natural tension of the occasion would permit. Garrick spoke a word or two to each, but was still busy putting the finishing touches on the preparations for the "entertainment," as he called it facetiously, which he had arranged.

"Before I put to the test a rather novel combination which I have arranged," began Garrick, when they had all been seated, "I want to say a few words about some of the discoveries I have already made in this remarkable case."

He paused a moment to make sure that he had our attention, but it was unnecessary. We were all hanging eagerly on his words.

"There is, I believe," he resumed slowly, "no crime that is ever without a clew. The slightest trace, even a drop of blood no larger than a pin-head, may suffice to convict a murderer. So may a single hair found on the clothing of a suspect. In this case," he added quickly, "it is the impression made by the hammer of a pistol on the shell of a cartridge which leads

Arthur B. Reeve

unescapably to one conclusion."

The idea was so startling that we followed Garrick's every word as if weighted with tremendous importance, as indeed it was in the clearing up of this mysterious affair.

"I have made a collection from time to time," he pursued, "of the various exploded cartridges, the bullets, and the weapons left behind by the perpetrator of the dastardly series of crimes, from the shooting of the stool pigeon of the police, Rena Taylor, and the stealing of Mr. Warrington's car, down to the peculiar events of last night up in the Ramapos and the running fight through the streets of New York in taxicabs this morning.

"I have studied this evidence with the microscope and the microphotographic apparatus. I have secured excellent microphotographs of the marks made by various weapons on the cartridges and bullets. Taking those used in the commission of the greater crimes in this series, I find that the marks are the same, apparently, whether the gun shot off a bullet of wax or tallow which became liquid in the body, whether it discharged a stupefying gas, or whether the deadly anaesthetic bullet was fired. I have obtained a gun"—he threw it on the table with a clang—"the marks from the hammer of which correspond with the marks made on all the cartridges I have mentioned. One person owned that gun and used it. That is proved. It remains only to connect that gun positively and definitely, as a last link, with that person."

I noticed with a start that the revolver still had a stout cord tied to it.

As he concluded, Garrick had begun fitting a curious little device to each of our forearms. It looked to me like an electrode consisting of large plates of German silver, covered with felt and saturated with salt solution. From each electrode wires ran across the floor to some hidden apparatus.

"Back of this screen," he went on, indicating it in the corner of the room, "I have placed what is known as the string galvanometer, invented, or, perhaps better, perfected by Dr. Einthoven, of Leyden. It was designed primarily for the study of the beating of the heart in cases of disease, but it also may be used to record and study emotions as well,— love and hate, fear, joy, anger, remorse, all are revealed by this uncanny, cold, ruthlessly scientific instrument.

"The machine is connected by wires to each of you, and will make what are called electrocardiographs, in which every emotion, every sentiment, every passion is recorded inevitably, inexorably. For, the electric current that passes from each of you to the machine over these wires carrying the record of the secrets of your hearts is one of the feeblest currents known to science. Yet it can be caught and measured. The dynamo which generates this current is not a huge affair of steel castings and endless windings of copper wire. It is merely the heart of the sitter.

"The heart makes only one three-thousandth of a volt of electricity at each beat. It would take thousands of hearts to light one electric light, hundreds of thousands to run one trolley car. Yet just that slight little current from the heart is enough to sway a gossamer strand of quartz fibre in what I may call my 'heart station' here. This current, as I have told you, passes from each of you over a wire and vibrates a fine quartz fibre in unison with it, one of the most delicate bits of mechanism ever made, recording the result on a photo-graphic film by means of a beam of light reflected from a delicate mirror."

We sat spellbound as Garrick unfolded the dreadful, awe-inspiring possibilities of the machine behind the screen. He walked slowly to the back of the room.

"Now, here I have one of the latest of the inventions of the Wizard of West Orange—Edison," he resumed. "It is, as you perhaps have already guessed, the latest product of this genius of sound and sight, the kinetophone, the machine that combines moving pictures with the talking machine."

A stranger stepped in from an outer office. He was the skilled operator of the kinetophone, whom Garrick had hired. In a few terse sentences he explained that back of a curtain which he pulled down before us was a phonograph with a megaphone, that from his booth behind us he operated the picture films, and that the two were absolutely synchronized.

A moment later a picture began to move on the screen. Sounds and voices seemed to emerge as if from the very screen itself. There, before us, we saw a gambling joint operating in full blast. It was not the Forty-eighth Street resort. But it was strongly reminiscent of it. From the talking machine proceeded all the noises familiar to such a scene.

Garrick had moved behind the screen that cut off our view of the galvanometer. One after another, he was studying the emotions of each of his audience.

Suddenly the scene changed. A door was burst in, cards and gambling paraphernalia were scattered about and hidden, men rushed to escape, and the sounds were much like those on the night of the raid. Garrick was still engrossed in the study of what the galvanometer was showing.

The film stopped. Without warning, the operator started another. It was a group of men and women playing cards. A man entered, and engaged in conversation with one of the women who was playing. They left the room.

The next scene was in an entirely different room. But the connection which was implied with the last scene was obvious. Different actors entered the room, a man and a woman. There was a dispute—there was a crack of a revolver—and the woman fell. People rushed in. Everything was done to hide the crime. The girl was carried out into a waiting automobile, propped in as if overcome by alcohol and whisked away. I found myself almost looking to see if the car was of the make of Warrington's, so great was the impression the scene made on me. Of course it was not, but it all seemed so real that one might be pardoned for expecting the impossible, especially when her body was thrown, with many a muttered imprecation, by the roadside, and in the last picture the man was cleaning the exploded gun. One single still picture followed. It was a huge, enlarged cartridge.

I followed the thing with eager eyes and ears. From a long list of canned and reeled plays, Garrick had selected here and there such scenes and acts as, interspersed with a few single, original pictures of his own, like the cartridge, would serve best to recapitulate the very case which we had been investigating. It carried me along step by step, wonderfully.

Another moving and talking picture was under way. This time it seemed to be a race between two automobiles. They were tearing along, and the sound of the rapidly working cylinders was most real. The rearmost was rapidly over-hauling that in front. Imagine our surprise as it crept up on the other to see the driver rise, whip out a pistol, and fire point blank at the other as he dashed ahead, and the picture stopped.

A suppressed scream escaped Violet Winslow. It was too

much like what had happened to Mortimer Warrington for her to repress the shudder that swept over her, and an involuntary movement toward him to make sure that it was not real.

Still Garrick did not move from his post at the galvanometer. He was taking no chances. He had us thrilled, tense, and he meant to take advantage to the full in reading the truth in the dramatic situation he had so skilfully created.

Another picture started almost on the heels of the last. It was of the robbery of a safe. Then came another, a firebug at work in starting a conflagration. We could hear the crackling of flames, the shouts of the people, the clang of bells, and the hasty tread of the firemen as they advanced and put out the blaze. The film play was one of those which never fail to attract, where the makers had gone to the utmost extent of realism and had actually set fire to a house to get the true effect.

The next was a scene from a detective play, pure and simple, in which that marvellous little instrument which had served us in such good stead in this case was played up strongly, the detectaphone. Then followed a scene from another play in which a young girl was kidnapped and rescued by her lover just in the nick of time. Nothing could have been selected to arouse the feelings of the little audience to a higher pitch.

The last of the series, which I knew was to be a climax, was not an American picture. It was quite evidently made in Paris and was from actual life. I myself had been startled when the title was announced by the voice and on the screen simultaneously, "The Siege of the Motor Bandits by the Paris Police."

It was terrific. It began with the shouts of the crowd urging on the police, the crack of revolvers and guns from a little house or garage in the suburbs, the advance and retreat of the gendarmes on the stronghold. Back and forth the battle waged. One could hear the sharp orders of the police, the shrill taunts of the bandits, the sounds of battle.

Then at a point where the bandits seemed to have beaten off the attack successfully, there came an automobile. From it I could see the police take an object which I now knew must be a Mathiot gun. The huge thing was set up and carefully aimed. Then with a dull roar it was fired.

We could see the bomb hurtling through the air, see it strike the little house with a cloud of smoke and dust, hear the report of the explosion, the shouts of dismay of the bandits— then silence. A cry went up from the crowd as the police now pressed forward in a mass and rushed into the house, disclosing the last scene—in which the bandits were suffocated.

The film suddenly stopped. Garrick's office, which had been ringing with firearms and shouts from the kinetophone, was again silent. It was an impressive silence, too. No one of us but had felt and lived the whole case over again in the brief time that the talking movies had been shown.

The lights flashed up, and before we realised that the thing was over, Garrick was standing before us, holding in his hand a long sheet of paper. The look on his face told plainly that his novel experiment had succeeded.

"I may say," he began, still studying the paper in his hand, although I knew he must have arrived at his conclusion already or he would never have quitted his "heart station," so soon, "I may say that some time ago a letter was sent to Miss Winslow purporting to reveal some of Mr. Warrington's alleged connections and escapades. It is needless to say that as far as the accusations were concerned he was able to meet them all adequately and, as for the innuendoes, they were pure baseless fabrications. The sender was urged on to do it by someone else who also had an interest of another kind in placing Mr. Warrington in a bad light with Miss Winslow. But the sender soon realised his mistake. The fact that he was willing to go to the length of a dangerous robbery accompanied by arson in order to get back or destroy the letter showed how afraid he was to have a sample of his handwriting fall into my hands. He blundered, but even then he did not realise how badly.

"For, in certain cases the handwriting shows a great deal more than would be recognised even by the ordinary handwriting expert. This letter showed that the writer was, as I have already explained to Mr. Marshall, the victim of a peculiar kind of paralysis which begins to show itself in nerve tremours for days before the attack and exhibits itself even in the handwriting."

"Now, my string galvanometer shows not only the effects of these moving and talking pictures on the emotions, but also, as it was really designed to do, the state of the heart with reference to normality. It shows to me plainly the effect of disease on the heart, even if it is latent in the subject. While I have been using the psychological law of suggestion, and have been recapitulating as well as I was able under the circumstances the whole story of the crime briefly in moving and talking pictures, I have found, in addition, that the same heart which shows the emotions I expected also shows the disease which I discovered in the blackmailing letter.

"There was surprise at the sight of the gambling den, rage at the raid, fear at the murder of the girl in the other den and the disposal of her body, excitement over the racing motor cars, passion over the kidnapping of the girl, anger over the little detectaphone, and panic at the siege of the bandits, as I showed by the selection of the films that I was getting closer and closer to the truth. And there was the same abnormality of the heart exhibited throughout."

Garrick paused. I scarcely breathed, nor did I move my eyes, which were riveted on his face. What was he going to reveal next? Was he going to accuse someone in the room?

"Mr. Marshall," he resumed with a smile toward me, "I am glad to say is quite normal and innocent of all wrongdoing— in this instance," he added with a momentary flash of humour. "Commissioner Dillon also passes muster. Mr. Warrington—I shall come back to, later."

I thought Violet Winslow gave a little, startled gasp. She turned toward him, anyhow, and I saw that not even science now could shake her faith in him.

"Mr. Forbes," he continued, speaking rapidly as I bent forward to catch every word, "incriminated himself quite sufficiently in connection with the gambling joint, the raid and the slanderous letter, so that I should advise him when this case comes to trial to tell the whole truth and nothing but the truth about his helping a gunman in order to further what proved a hopeless love affair on his own part. Here, too, is a little vest-pocket gun that was found under such circumstances as would be likely to connect Forbes in the popular mind with the shootings."

"My lawyer has my statement about that. I'll read—"

"No, Forbes," interrupted Garrick. "You needn't read. Your lawyer may be interested to add this to the statement, however. A pistol that has been shot off has potassium sulphide from the powder in the barrel. Later, it oxidizes and iron oxide is found. This weapon has neither the sulphide nor the oxide, as far as I can determine. It has never even been discharged. No, it was not the pistol found on Forbes that figured in this case.

"As far as that new-fangled gun goes, Forbes, it was a frame-up. You were kidnapped by a man whom you thought was your friend, and it was done for a purpose. He knew the situation you were in, your jealousy—I won't dwell on that here. He held you at the house up in the valley. You told the truth about that. He did it, the man who wrote the letter, because he hoped ultimately to shift all the guilt on you and himself go scot-free."

Forbes stared dumbly. I knew he had known what was coming but had held back for fear of what he knew had always happened to informers in the circle to which he had sunk.

"McBirney," continued Garrick, "your emotions, mostly astonishment, show that you have much to learn in this new business of modern detection, besides the recovery of stolen cars."

Garrick had paused for effect again.

"And now we come to the keeper of a nighthawk garage on the West Side, a man whom they seem to call the Boss. That is getting higher up. I find that he points, according to this scientific third degree, to one whom I have for a long time suspected—"

A dull thud startled us.

I turned. A man was lying, face down, on the floor.

Before any of us could reach him, Garrick concluded, "This is the man who framed up the case against Forbes, who stole Warrington's car to use to get rid of the body of the informer, Rena Taylor, because she by her success interfered with his gambling graft, who wrote the letter to Miss Winslow to injure Warrington because he, too, was interfering with his graft collection from the gambling house by threatening to close it up. He committed the arson to cover up his identity by getting back the letter; he planned and nearly executed the kidnapping of Miss Winslow in order to hold up Warrington, and then hid in the country where we ferreted him out, not far from the very scene of a murderous attack on Warrington for his brave stand in suppressing gambling—from which this man was weekly shaking down a huge profit as the price of police protection of the vice."

Garrick was kneeling by the prostrate form now, not so much the accuser as the scientist, studying a new phase of crime.

The threatened paralysis had struck Inspector Herman sooner than even Garrick had expected.

When we had made Herman as comfortable as we could, Garrick added to Dillon, who stood over us, speechless, "You had under you one of the strong links in the secret system of police protection of vice and crime, and you never knew it—the greatest grafter and scientific gunman that I ever knew. It has been a long, hard fight. But I have the goods on him at last."

The exposure was startling in the extreme. Herman had gained for himself the reputation of being one of the shrewdest and most efficient men in the department. But he had felt the lure of graft. With the aid of the gamblers and unscrupulous politicians he had built up a huge, secret machine for collection of the profits from the sale of police protection against the enforcement of the law he was sworn to uphold.

He had begun to mix with doubtful characters. But he was a genius and had become, by degrees, the worst of the gangmen and gunmen who ever operated in the metropolis. Detailed to catch the gamblers and gangsters, with official power to do almost as he pleased, he had enjoyed a fine holiday and employed his leisure both for new crimes and in covering up so successfully his tracks in the old ones, even with Garrick on his trail, that he had been able to completely hoodwink his superior, Dillon, by his long, detailed reports which sounded very convincing but which really meant nothing.

As the strange truth of the case was established by Garrick, Dillon was the most amazed of us all. He had trusted Herman, and the revulsion of feeling was overwhelming.

"And to think," he exclaimed, in disgust, "that I actually placed his own case in his own hands, with carte blanche instructions to go ahead. No wonder he never produced a clew that amounted to anything. Well, I'll be—"

Words failed him, as he looked down and glared savagely at the man in silence.

All were now crowding around Garrick eager to thank him for what he had done. As Warrington, now almost his former hearty wholesome self again, grasped Garrick's hand in the heartiness of his thanks, Garrick, with the electrocardiogram paper still in his other hand, smiled.

He released himself and turned to touch the dainty little hand of Violet Winslow, whose eyes were so full of happy tears that she could scarcely speak.

"Miss Winslow," he beamed, gazing earnestly and admiringly into her sweet face, "I promised to attend to the case of that man later,—" he added, with a nod at Warrington. "It may interest you to know scientifically what you already know by something that is greater than science, a woman's intuition."

She blushed as he added, "Mr. Warrington has a good, strong, healthy heart. He wouldn't be alive to-day if he hadn't. But, more than that, I have observed throughout the evening that he has hardly taken his eyes off you. Even the 'talkies' and the 'movies' failed to stir him until the kidnapping scene overwhelmed him. Here on this strip of paper I have a billet-doux. His heart registers the current that only that consummate electrician, little Dan Cupid, can explain."

ABOUT THE AUTHOR

Arthur Benjamin Reeve (October 15, 1880 - August 9, 1936) was an American mystery writer. He is best known for creating the series character Professor Craig Kennedy, sometimes called "The American Sherlock Holmes," and his Dr Watson-like sidekick Walter Jameson, a newspaper reporter, in eighteen detective novels. The bulk of Reeve's fame is based on the 82 Craig Kennedy stories, published in Cosmopolitan magazine between 1910 and 1918.

He graduated from Princeton and attended New York Law School. He worked as an editor and journalist before Craig Kennedy propelled him to national fame in 1911. Raised in Brooklyn, he lived most of his professional life at various addresses near the Long Island Sound.

Starting with The Exploits of Elaine (1914), Reeve began authoring screenplays. His film career reached its peak in 1919-20, when his name appeared on seven films, most of them serials, three of them starring Harry Houdini.

In the 1930's, Reeve rejuvenated his career by becoming an anti-rackets crusader. He had a national radio show from July 1930 to March 1931; he published a history of the rackets titled The Golden Age of Crime; and the focus of his Craig Kennedy stories completed the transition from "scientific detective" work to a racket-busting milieu.

Other books by this author

Constance Dunlap

The Gold of the Gods

The Master Mystery

The Film Mystery

The Exploits of Elaine

Arthur B. Reeve

Choose from Thousands of 1stWorldLibrary Classics By

A. M. Barnard
Ada Leverson
Adolphus William Ward
Aesop
Agatha Christie
Alexander Aaronsohn
Alexander Kielland
Alexandre Dumas
Alfred Gatty
Alfred Ollivant
Alice Duer Miller
Alice Turner Curtis
Alice Dunbar
Allen Chapman
Alleyne Ireland
Ambrose Bierce
Amelia E. Barr
Amory H. Bradford
Andrew Lang
Andrew McFarland Davis
Andy Adams
Angela Brazil
Anna Alice Chapin
Anna Sewell
Annie Besant
Annie Hamilton Donnell
Annie Payson Call
Annie Roe Carr
Annonaymous
Anton Chekhov
Archibald Lee Fletcher
Arnold Bennett
Arthur C. Benson
Arthur Conan Doyle
Arthur M. Winfield
Arthur Ransome
Arthur Schnitzler
Arthur Train
Atticus
B.H. Baden-Powell
B. M. Bower
B. C. Chatterjee
Baroness Emmuska Orczy
Baroness Orczy
Basil King
Bayard Taylor
Ben Macomber
Bertha Muzzy Bower
Bjornstjerne Bjornson

Booth Tarkington
Boyd Cable
Bram Stoker
C. Collodi
C. E. Orr
C. M. Ingleby
Carolyn Wells
Catherine Parr Traill
Charles A. Eastman
Charles Amory Beach
Charles Dickens
Charles Dudley Warner
Charles Farrar Browne
Charles Ives
Charles Kingsley
Charles Klein
Charles Hanson Towne
Charles Lathrop Pack
Charles Romyn Dake
Charles Whibley
Charles Willing Beale
Charlotte M. Braeme
Charlotte M. Yonge
Charlotte Perkins Stetson
Clair W. Hayes
Clarence Day Jr.
Clarence E. Mulford
Clemence Housman
Confucius
Coningsby Dawson
Cornelis DeWitt Wilcox
Cyril Burleigh
D. H. Lawrence
Daniel Defoe
David Garnett
Dinah Craik
Don Carlos Janes
Donald Keyhoe
Dorothy Kilner
Dougan Clark
Douglas Fairbanks
E. Nesbit
E. P. Roe
E. Phillips Oppenheim
E. S. Brooks
Earl Barnes
Edgar Rice Burroughs
Edith Van Dyne
Edith Wharton

Edward Everett Hale
Edward J. O'Biren
Edward S. Ellis
Edwin L. Arnold
Eleanor Atkins
Eleanor Hallowell Abbott
Eliot Gregory
Elizabeth Gaskell
Elizabeth McCracken
Elizabeth Von Arnim
Ellem Key
Emerson Hough
Emilie F. Carlen
Emily Bronte
Emily Dickinson
Enid Bagnold
Enilor Macartney Lane
Erasmus W. Jones
Ernie Howard Pie
Ethel May Dell
Ethel Turner
Ethel Watts Mumford
Eugene Sue
Eugenie Foa
Eugene Wood
Eustace Hale Ball
Evelyn Everett-green
Everard Cotes
F. H. Cheley
F. J. Cross
F. Marion Crawford
Fannie E. Newberry
Federick Austin Ogg
Ferdinand Ossendowski
Fergus Hume
Florence A. Kilpatrick
Fremont B. Deering
Francis Bacon
Francis Darwin
Frances Hodgson Burnett
Frances Parkinson Keyes
Frank Gee Patchin
Frank Harris
Frank Jewett Mather
Frank L. Packard
Frank V. Webster
Frederic Stewart Isham
Frederick Trevor Hill
Frederick Winslow Taylor

Friedrich Kerst
Friedrich Nietzsche
Fyodor Dostoyevsky
G.A. Henty
G.K. Chesterton
Gabrielle E. Jackson
Garrett P. Serviss
Gaston Leroux
George A. Warren
George Ade
Geroge Bernard Shaw
George Cary Eggleston
George Durston
George Ebers
George Eliot
George Gissing
George MacDonald
George Meredith
George Orwell
George Sylvester Viereck
George Tucker
George W. Cable
George Wharton James
Gertrude Atherton
Gordon Casserly
Grace E. King
Grace Gallatin
Grace Greenwood
Grant Allen
Guillermo A. Sherwell
Gulielma Zollinger
Gustav Flaubert
H. A. Cody
H. B. Irving
H. C. Bailey
H. G. Wells
H. H. Munro
H. Irving Hancock
H. R. Naylor
H. Rider Haggard
H. W. C. Davis
Haldeman Julius
Hall Caine
Hamilton Wright Mabie
Hans Christian Andersen
Harold Avery
Harold McGrath
Harriet Beecher Stowe
Harry Castlemon
Harry Coghill
Harry Houidini

Hayden Carruth
Helent Hunt Jackson
Helen Nicolay
Hendrik Conscience
Hendy David Thoreau
Henri Barbusse
Henrik Ibsen
Henry Adams
Henry Ford
Henry Frost
Henry James
Henry Jones Ford
Henry Seton Merriman
Henry W Longfellow
Herbert A. Giles
Herbert Carter
Herbert N. Casson
Herman Hesse
Hildegard G. Frey
Homer
Honore De Balzac
Horace B. Day
Horace Walpole
Horatio Alger Jr.
Howard Pyle
Howard R. Garis
Hugh Lofting
Hugh Walpole
Humphry Ward
Ian Maclaren
Inez Haynes Gillmore
Irving Bacheller
Isabel Cecilia Williams
Isabel Hornibrook
Israel Abrahams
Ivan Turgenev
J. G.Austin
J. Henri Fabre
J. M. Barrie
J. M. Walsh
J. Macdonald Oxley
J. R. Miller
J. S. Fletcher
J. S. Knowles
J. Storer Clouston
J. W. Duffield
Jack London
Jacob Abbott
James Allen
James Andrews
James Baldwin

James Branch Cabell
James DeMille
James Joyce
James Lane Allen
James Lane Allen
James Oliver Curwood
James Oppenheim
James Otis
James R. Driscoll
Jane Abbott
Jane Austen
Jane L. Stewart
Janet Aldridge
Jens Peter Jacobsen
Jerome K. Jerome
Jessie Graham Flower
John Buchan
John Burroughs
John Cournos
John F. Kennedy
John Gay
John Glasworthy
John Habberton
John Joy Bell
John Kendrick Bangs
John Milton
John Philip Sousa
John Taintor Foote
Jonas Lauritz Idemil Lie
Jonathan Swift
Joseph A. Altsheler
Joseph Carey
Joseph Conrad
Joseph E. Badger Jr
Joseph Hergesheimer
Joseph Jacobs
Jules Vernes
Julian Hawthrone
Julie A Lippmann
Justin Huntly McCarthy
Kakuzo Okakura
Karle Wilson Baker
Kate Chopin
Kenneth Grahame
Kenneth McGaffey
Kate Langley Bosher
Kate Langley Bosher
Katherine Cecil Thurston
Katherine Stokes
L. A. Abbot
L. T. Meade

L. Frank Baum
Latta Griswold
Laura Dent Crane
Laura Lee Hope
Laurence Housman
Lawrence Beasley
Leo Tolstoy
Leonid Andreyev
Lewis Carroll
Lewis Sperry Chafer
Lilian Bell
Lloyd Osbourne
Louis Hughes
Louis Joseph Vance
Louis Tracy
Louisa May Alcott
Lucy Fitch Perkins
Lucy Maud Montgomery
Luther Benson
Lydia Miller Middleton
Lyndon Orr
M. Corvus
M. H. Adams
Margaret E. Sangster
Margret Howth
Margaret Vandercook
Margaret W. Hungerford
Margret Penrose
Maria Edgeworth
Maria Thompson Daviess
Mariano Azuela
Marion Polk Angellotti
Mark Overton
Mark Twain
Mary Austin
Mary Catherine Crowley
Mary Cole
Mary Hastings Bradley
Mary Roberts Rinehart
Mary Rowlandson
M. Wollstonecraft Shelley
Maud Lindsay
Max Beerbohm
Myra Kelly
Nathaniel Hawthrone
Nicolo Machiavelli
O. F. Walton
Oscar Wilde
Owen Johnson
P.G. Wodehouse
Paul and Mabel Thorne

Paul G. Tomlinson
Paul Severing
Percy Brebner
Percy Keese Fitzhugh
Peter B. Kyne
Plato
Quincy Allen
R. Derby Holmes
R. L. Stevenson
R. S. Ball
Rabindranath Tagore
Rahul Alvares
Ralph Bonehill
Ralph Henry Barbour
Ralph Victor
Ralph Waldo Emmerson
Rene Descartes
Ray Cummings
Rex Beach
Rex E. Beach
Richard Harding Davis
Richard Jefferies
Richard Le Gallienne
Robert Barr
Robert Frost
Robert Gordon Anderson
Robert L. Drake
Robert Lansing
Robert Lynd
Robert Michael Ballantyne
Robert W. Chambers
Rosa Nouchette Carey
Rudyard Kipling
Saint Augustine
Samuel B. Allison
Samuel Hopkins Adams
Sarah Bernhardt
Sarah C. Hallowell
Selma Lagerlof
Sherwood Anderson
Sigmund Freud
Standish O'Grady
Stanley Weyman
Stella Benson
Stella M. Francis
Stephen Crane
Stewart Edward White
Stijn Streuvels
Swami Abhedananda
Swami Parmananda
T. S. Ackland

T. S. Arthur
The Princess Der Ling
Thomas A. Janvier
Thomas A Kempis
Thomas Anderton
Thomas Bailey Aldrich
Thomas Bulfinch
Thomas De Quincey
Thomas Dixon
Thomas H. Huxley
Thomas Hardy
Thomas More
Thornton W. Burgess
U. S. Grant
Upton Sinclair
Valentine Williams
Various Authors
Vaughan Kester
Victor Appleton
Victor G. Durham
Victoria Cross
Virginia Woolf
Wadsworth Camp
Walter Camp
Walter Scott
Washington Irving
Wilbur Lawton
Wilkie Collins
Willa Cather
Willard F. Baker
William Dean Howells
William le Queux
W. Makepeace Thackeray
William W. Walter
William Shakespeare
Winston Churchill
Yei Theodora Ozaki
Yogi Ramacharaka
Young E. Allison
Zane Grey

www.ingramcontent.com/pod-product-compliance
Lightning Source LLC
Chambersburg PA
CBHW030121180626
46812CB00002B/514

* 9 7 8 1 4 2 1 8 8 8 1 1 8 *